"Tell me more about what you do," I asked, wanting to find out more about this nice-looking agent.

"I deal with maintaining national security," he said.

"That's pretty vague. Can you tell me anything more?" I prompted.

"My job is protecting and maintaining the security of agency assets and personnel."

"So, am I your first?" I added just to be funny. For some reason, I felt compelled to verbally spar with him a bit.

"Excuse me - first what?" He looked like he was going to swallow his tongue.

From his expression, I knew what he was thinking. "The first person you've had to protect. Have you been in this kind of situation before?" I turned toward him to see what he'd say.

Handguns and Honeymoons

Anne K. Nagel

Nagela Press

Anchorage

Library of Congress Control Number 2018914927
ISBN 978-0-9889676-1-8

Published in the United States by Nagela Press,
P.O. Box 210036, Anchorage, Alaska, 99521-0036.

The publisher is not responsible for websites or website contents that are not owned by the publisher.

To Ivan and Aaron, for the information and guidance.

To Beth and Justin, for the encouragement and the kick in the pants when it was needed.

And to the readers, to inspire them to dare to try.

Chapter 1

A single question can change everything. The problem is, once I asked that question, the answers altered my perspective and nothing was ever the same again. Knowledge creates a one-way transformation. Life is dangerous without it, but I have discovered that it is impossible to return to the way I imagined things were before.

I'll never forget what started it off. I stepped down a drab hallway at work with my ordinary, low-heeled shoes and a typical, unpretentious wardrobe expecting a usual day.

The guys normally talk about their camping and fishing trips. The younger ones may talk about going to a bar or a concert. Today, they were all talking about something on the news. Some sort of data theft had occurred.

Great; that probably meant more training on data security in our futures. I was extremely concerned in case something like that might happen to us. As a civilian federal employee working for surveyors, my duties may have seemed nondescript to anyone else. My job was researching the records for accuracy and inputting the data painstakingly into the survey database. I was good at my job and I took it seriously. I certainly didn't like the idea of someone tampering with what I considered to be my data. My innate inclination to solve problems and search for answers was what changed my future and got me in trouble. I didn't know it then, but I was just the right person at the right place at the right time… or the wrong time, depending upon how you choose to look at it.

As I continued on down toward my cubicle, I passed by Arty Justman's area. He was one of the older surveyors who always seemed to be rubbing somebody the wrong way.

The screens of the cubicles don't block out much sound. It was easy to hear that Arty wasn't very happy with somebody on the phone. He spoke forcefully, "You told me to go to the site and look around. I was paid to find this piece of technology, but you didn't pay me enough to do a complete excavation of the entire area. I've always passed on all there was. No other wreckage was found!"

Hiring a federal employee to perform private work could be questionable. I knew he was frequently strapped for cash since I'd overheard him at times ranting to his wife about spending too much. Being older, he was probably planning for retirement as well.

The cranky surveyor hastily interrupted whoever was on the other end of the line. "I have done what you wanted! Believe me! I gave the last object I found to Evanston, just like you said." His tone turned desperate. "I would have delivered this to him, too, but you guys changed things. What's going on? Why are you altering the procedures now?" There was a pause and he sputtered, "What do you mean, you'll deal with him?"

Arty rarely backed down from anyone. Yet he didn't seem willing to antagonize the person on the phone. That was out of character. This caller certainly had Arty intimidated.

Then I heard the irascible surveyor loudly say, "They're here now? You're checking up on me?" Arty turned away to pick up an object and stuff it into a pocket of his baggy old cardigan. What I could see of it, the thing wasn't too big and had receptacles on one end, much like you'd find on a nine-volt battery. That's the joy of having cubicles; there's no privacy.

He stormed out of his cubicle just as I went on my way. Fortunately, he stomped off in the opposite direction. In his anger he didn't even notice me.

I didn't have much time to mull over what I'd seen and heard because once I got to my cubicle, I got a call from Sara, the records clerk.

"I'm trying to help a couple of very demanding customers, and our system is down. IT is working on it, but it'll take too long and these men want it now. They insist they can't wait. I need everything done by surveyor Arty Justman on 2 North, 12 West, Seward. Could you bring it down to me? Please, Gia? I'll owe you one," she asked.

That was the area where Arty was working. Someone on the phone was riding Arty about something, and now these men downstairs wanted information on his surveys. Coincidences like that just don't happen in real life. Those thoughts troubled me as I grabbed the printouts and quickly went downstairs to help her with these unusually demanding people.

When I got to the records center, I noted the men who were talking with Sara. People from the general public who come to ask for survey information don't usually wear expensive-looking suits. The typical customers are land managers or surveyors, and they dress casually. With their tailored clothes, the two could possibly be a couple high-end lawyers.

Sara gave me a grateful smile when I delivered the printouts. I let her give them to her customers because it didn't bother me if she got the credit.

Eventually, her difficult customers' demands were satisfied. As they were paying for their printouts, she whispered to me "I'm so relieved that they can go on their way. Thank you so much." I smiled at her and hurried back upstairs.

***

As I made my way back to my desk, I thought about what I'd learned. I asked some of the surveyors, just to see if they might know anything about the object I'd seen. Will, a friendly young surveyor, didn't mind sharing information when he could. He showed me some instrument catalogs. We originally thought that Arty's interesting object could be a new version of an inertial positioning system. He couldn't find anything that resembled the device at all.

This was curious and I pondered the situation for a while. My thoughts were interrupted when the phone rang. The phone prefix indicated it was another government number.

"My name is Simeon," the deep voice on the line said, "I need to find some information. Can you tell me about the surveys done by surveyor Arty Justman on Township 2 North, Range 12 West, Seward?" His voice carried a hint of command.

All the interest concerning Arty's surveys seemed unusual and heightened my curiosity. "I can get that information for you, no problem, since you're calling from another federal number. We're supposed to help other government employees, but I don't recognize the caller I.D. Which agency is this?"

"National Security Agency," was his terse explanation. "I really need to know about those surveys. I'll be by shortly to take a look at what you've got." He said his thanks and hung up.

Arty passed by as I was on the phone. He hung around, watching that I had written down the familiar township and range. Hoping he'd move along, I ignored him. He still stood there.

When I looked up, he demanded, "Someone mentioned you had seen me with an object. Who else did you tell?" He gave me another one of those sour looks that makes me feel like I'm doing something wrong. I couldn't help wondering what the crotchety old man might have gotten into this time.

"I just asked if it might be an instrument the guys use, but Will couldn't find anything that looked like it."

Arty leaned over my desk and heatedly said, "You get too curious, and you'll get into trouble, and get young Will in trouble, too." His reaction was out of the ordinary, even for grouchy Arty.

As he stormed off, I muttered, "There must be something fishy about that object I saw." At the time, I didn't realize the serious consequences of what I had set in motion.

***

Later that day, I began running low on energy. It was time for an espresso.

With coffee in hand, I had rounded the corner to get back to my small, sparsely decorated cubicle. I noticed somebody standing by my area like he was waiting for me. That was unusual because the surveyors in my section just drop off anything to be input and leave.

My attention to detail kicked in. He was a good looking guy. That wasn't hard to pick out. His dark brown hair was short compared to the free-and-easy style the surveyors in the office usually wear. It had just a few wisps of gray at the temples, which made him look very dashing. His expression indicated he had a lot on his mind, so I could almost forgive the fact that the tall stranger was looming over my domain.

The interloper was very fit and trim, clean-shaved with a slight tan that hinted at outdoor activities. Most of the surveyors sport beards to protect their faces from the bugs and the elements when they are out working. While the surveyors are a casual bunch of guys, the serious set to this visitor's jaw and the lines around his green eyes got me to wondering what kind of a job could make a person that intense.

This non-surveyor didn't wear the universal jeans or outdoor work clothes all the surveyors seem to prefer. His suit was crisp and pressed. It was clear he had business to conduct, so I decided to cut him a little slack and find out what he needed.

"Hello, I'm Gia. May I help you?" I greeted him.

His gaze took an immediate assessment of me, from my not-quite-brown, not-quite-blonde hair to my somewhat-blue, somewhat-gray eyes. I figured he probably saw an unremarkable employee of average height, dressed in inconspicuous office clothes in neutral colors. Would his evaluation conclude that my abilities were as unexceptional as my appearance? For some reason, I hoped that wouldn't be the case.

Reaching into his pocket, the man brought out government identification that showed he was with NSA. As he flashed his credentials, he introduced himself. "Agent John Simeon, in the Division of Cryptologic Cyber Planning." He offered his hand and shook mine with a firm grip. My heartrate sped up. I've never had that happen before.

He remarked, "I spoke with someone about some surveys. Was that you?"

"Yes. I remember you called. Would you care to have a seat?" I offered, pointing to an extra chair.

The agent took off his suit jacket. He laid it on the back of the chair and sat down. The way this guy's shirt was pulled flat across his torso, I couldn't help but notice that he had a six-pack under there.

I almost sighed, but covered it by taking a sip from my coffee cup. Once I got myself together I asked, "What is

Cryptologic Cyber Planning, and why does your agency want this survey information?"

Mr. Simeon continued on, answering my first question, but ignoring the second. "NSA is concerned with understanding who, what, and where a potential threat comes from, and providing knowledge and safeguards against that danger. Cryptologic Cyber Planning deals with developing procedures that support Cyber Operations and Security. What do you do around here?" He got right to the issue.

"I input and verify survey data. But what is the issue with this particular survey information?"

Just then my phone rang. I saw the caller I.D. and made an apology since it was my boss. He told me to expect a federal agent asking about some surveys.

"Yes, he's here now," I told my supervisor. "Yes, I am giving him complete cooperation, don't worry." Isn't that just like bureaucracy? It's always a little late and a little lacking in specifics when giving instructions! Hanging up, I turned my attention back to the agent.

"What can people see when they ask for a specific survey?" he asked as he showed me a number.

"That's one of Arty Justman's surveys," I said with dismay at the thought that one of the people I worked with might have been in trouble.

The agent gave a nod and said, "Yes, I understand it is. Can you get me more specific information about that survey?"

"Some other people were asking about that particular survey information, too. I'll start printing out the data for you." I sat down to use the computer.

He seemed quite intent on looking over my shoulder to see all the log-in procedures. I definitely didn't mind having a nice looking and good smelling guy standing close to me. However, he'd have to have a digital play-back in slow motion to see all the security protocols and menu selections I whizzed through, thanks to the double-shot espresso.

Something told me this agent's request tied in with all the other strange things I had noticed. Instead of displaying the information, the computer flashed a message saying *no data found.* That was unexpected.

"How is this possible?" I blew out a breath and asked the agent, "This is in 2 North, 12 West, Seward, isn't it? The township information is there, but not this specific survey."

I was motivated to do further checking, since the validity of my data was at stake. "If you don't mind, give me a few minutes to verify this. I know this was here earlier because some other people asked for it. This can't be right," I insisted.

He followed me as I checked the file storage area. "The file is missing, too. I can't believe the surveyors would do this," I said.

"They didn't want you to find it," the agent surmised.

I had to ask, "They? Who are these people you're talking about, and why would they want this information deleted?"

He leaned forward and said quietly, "I've been investigating an information syndicate. We've learned they've been planning something. This may be related to it."

It wasn't easy to wrap my brain around what he'd told me. "So, you mean they're hackers?"

He speared me with a serious gaze. "Hackers just steal data. The syndicate I've been following is called Ravens Eye Group. These guys will find and leak incriminating information or plant false stories to create chaos and gain leverage. They steal corporate technical data or government intelligence to destabilize any government or business that won't give them what they want. They don't mind destroying any individuals who refuse to give in to their demands."

"Why would they be deleting survey files? Anyone can see them. They aren't secret. The information can be replaced by our IT department. They take backups every 24 hours." I was at a loss to understand why it would be of such concern to these bad guys, since I could inform my boss and the missing data would be restored.

"In any computer situation, there is a delay till the IT people can get backup information retrieved. They've done this kind of thing before. This is just misdirection to keep something from being noticed immediately."

That made sense, from what I knew of how backup storage was handled. "Why haven't I heard of this group before?"

"Ravens Eye has recently come to the NSA's attention. So far, they're still relatively localized, but each successful tech theft, or bunch of bots they plant to multiply false data, teaches them deadlier tricks. Be glad you haven't run into these guys before," he said.

"How does Arty factor into all this?" I had to know.

"At this point, that remains to be seen. Tell me more about the other people asking about this same area."

"There were some insistent men downstairs, demanding the same printouts."

The agent was interested in that information, and nodded for me to continue.

"Well, they stood out because the people usually asking for survey data don't wear such expensive suits," I told him. "As I recall, they seemed to be checking up on him."

"Checking up on him?"

"Yes, Arty also accused somebody on the phone of doing that. Then the two pushy guys were asking for information on the surveys he's done." I couldn't think of anything else to add. His undivided attention was a little overwhelming.

"If I showed you some pictures, could you identify the men you saw?"

"Yes, I'd remember them. I'd be happy to help all I can. After all, we're supposed to cooperate with other government agencies."

This man's intense gaze made me so nervous in a way I'd never felt before. Was it fear, or excitement?

My desk phone had rung while I was showing the agent our files. The message light was flashing now. The caller I.D. indicated it was from one of the surveyors. If they were calling me, it was probably important. It might also have some bearing on the agent's requested information. Since he was busy looking at printouts, I anxiously took a moment to check the voice mails.

Will, the young surveyor, had left a message. "Hey, Gia, We're out here on a new survey and you'll never believe what I found. It turned out to be pieces of some sort of U.S. Government equipment. Probably one of those remote control drones you hear about in the news. One of the parts looks like what you were asking about," he said. "Your description is identical to what I'm seeing. I'll take some pictures to show you when I'm back in the office, but I'm not going to take anything with me. Those military guys can get pretty touchy. There are some guys here now who are getting pretty angry with us. Talk to you later."

Just before the message ended, I thought I heard a couple pops in the background and some yelling.

The agent noticed that I'd gone pale and had hung up the phone with trembling hands. He brazenly reached over to replay the message so he could listen to it as well.

As the message ended, he whipped out his cell phone and dialed. Talking to the person on the other end he said, "This is Agent Simeon. Let me talk to someone in Cyber Ops." He must have gotten through to the person there at this group. He looked at me and stated, "There's a new wrinkle."

"I'm probably part of that wrinkle," I muttered. When he noticed that I caught him looking at me, he quickly stepped away to finish his conversation.

In a few minutes, he walked back to my desk. "It would be better if you get your things and come with me," he said apologetically. He grabbed his jacket to leave.

"Maybe you'd better talk to my supervisor first," I suggested, almost hopeful that my supervisor would decline.

"What is the person's number?" He called the number and I was able to listen in to the agent's side of the conversation.

"Yes, she needs to come now. No, she isn't in trouble; this is part of an on-going investigation. Good, I'm glad to have your cooperation." The victorious agent thumbed his phone off at that.

"There's more to this than you've told me, isn't there?" Getting my coat, I worried about what I'd gotten entangled in now.

The agent just hurried me along. The more closed-lipped he got, the more troubled I became. Somehow, it never occurred to me to dig my heels in.

It was late afternoon as we went out to his car. "Of course, you have to have a sporty red one," I laughed nervously in this unfamiliar situation. "You still need to explain to me what's going on."

"Relax. You'll take a look at some photos and be on your way," he assured me.

We made it to an unremarkable building, and we parked. After going through some pretty thorough security, he led me inside. We stepped into a vacant conference room and he motioned for me to sit down.

I waited while he brought out a tablet and accessed a secure Wi-Fi connection so I could identify the men I had seen.

Thumbing through the pictures displayed on the device, I pointed at two of them. "Those two were the ones I saw downstairs asking for information on Arty's surveys."

"Tell me more about this object the surveyor was speaking about in that phone message."

"I don't know what it was. Arty got upset that they were apparently checking up on him and changed procedures. Then, he took this strange object out of his desk and left. It looked like it would be plugged in somewhere, though I couldn't see it very well."

The agent looked very concerned. "I figured as much. They were double-checking the information one of their informants was giving them. They were probably unhappy that Arty hadn't delivered the object yet."

"Is Arty their informant?"

"He's one of them." He paused to make a decision. "Thank you for the help. I appreciate your time. Did you leave your car at work?"

"Today I carpooled. By now the driver has probably left for the evening."

He insisted, "I'll drive you home." His manner suggested he usually got his way.

We sat in silence on the way to my apartment. Before we could head into the building, he reached behind his seat and brought out a black leather coat.

"It isn't necessary to walk me straight to my door." I didn't want to cause him any trouble.

He adjusted his heavy coat and continued.

I surmised, "You're going to do it anyway. Do you always get your way?"

He just gave me a small nod and said, "When it comes to keeping someone safe, I expect to."

That made me pause for a second and I stared at him.

He put his hand at my back to urge me along and we walked down the hall toward my apartment door. The smells of the other tenants' evening meals drifted through the building.

As I reached out to put the key in the knob, my door swung open. "I know I didn't leave it unlocked this morning," I insisted.

Agent Simeon quickly put a hand on my elbow to keep me from entering. He shifted us both away from the front of the door. He looked around and listened intently in case somebody was still there. His tone was deadly serious as he said, "Stay put." He drew a huge pistol and quietly entered the apartment. He carefully tracked his gun around every corner in every room.

I hadn't realized he'd had that weapon in his leather coat. That's why he put it on.

He went through the entire place. Once he was satisfied that no one was in my apartment, he lowered his weapon and stood guard, motioning for me to come in.

For some reason I told him, "I've seen people on those cop shows do that as they enter a room. It's interesting to see it actually done in real life."

He stayed vigilant. In his authoritative manner he inquired, "Look around. Have they taken anything?"

I did as he directed. "No. Everything looks..." I hesitated. "Wait. My thumb drives have all been moved. They aren't the way I left them."

"They probably didn't want to take anything. They may have bugged the place. Be careful what you say. These guys could copy your data and load a key logging program on your computer to learn more about you, so don't use it." He holstered his weapon and looked around.

I scanned the rest of my apartment, wondering what this handsome stranger would make of it. Suddenly everything about my life seemed mundane and uninteresting. "So, now they know things about me? I've only known you for a matter of hours, and my life is turned upside down!" I groused.

"Just stay calm," the agent told me.

"If this isn't time to panic, I don't want to be around when it is time!"

His phone rang. He walked outside the apartment to talk.

Without thinking, I turned on the TV. I lowered the volume and just zoned out for a while. One of the national news channels was on, talking about a raid somewhere. I'd been too late tuning in to get where that had taken place. My attention was caught as the words *recent data theft* scrolled by beneath the news commentators.

When the words *missing tech* appeared on the screen, I was frozen. I tried to piece together the strange occurrences with Arty, the missing survey data at work, and now the incident at my place. What could those people have expected to find in my apartment? Was this latest news on TV related to my break-in, too? What kind of a mess had I gotten myself into?

Looking out the window, I watched as the shadows crept over the landscape. Every move of the tree limbs became furtive, every sway of the bushes around my first-floor apartment seemed sinister.

Chapter 2

There, by the window, I became overwhelmed with a feeling of vulnerability. I had always counted on privacy and security, and I felt violated. My perspective shifted. The things that were once so ordinary and normal suddenly became menacing. Closing the blinds tight, I shivered and turned back to where Agent Simeon was talking on his phone.

The agent looked even more worried. His lips formed a tight line on his face as he ended his phone call. I didn't know if he was reacting to my obvious fear or the worsening situation.

"I know this is upsetting, but you don't have to face this by yourself. For now, throw some things together and I'll get you away from here. Later, if you're up for it, we'll talk, but we can't do that here," he said with a look of empathy.

His concern made me feel a little better. Something in his manner indicated I was in the middle of something bad. That's probably why I agreed to go with him in the first place. In this unfamiliar situation, I wondered if it would be worse to follow his instructions or stay in my apartment by myself. The mental picture of me being all alone in case the bad guys came back convinced me. That, and there was definitely something in his manner that indicated he expected others to follow his lead.

I turned to switch off the TV. Agent Simeon came up to watch the scrolling news captions as the broadcast showed a suave guy in handcuffs being led off. The caption changed to *deeper implications as data leak widens.*

The quick video of the man being put in a vehicle showed someone who might have been of Spanish, Mediterranean, or even Mid-Eastern descent. I turned up the volume, and the announcer talked about the "Alleged information broker arrested in the latest data theft scandal." When I remarked on it, the agent just said, "Hmm, looks like they got another bad guy."

"Is he with Ravens Eye?" I had to ask.

"Looks like it," was all he'd say.

Filing that away in my mind for later, I hurried into the bedroom and planned what I would need. As I threw a few things into an overnight bag, I asked, "Just where am I supposed to go?"

"I'm taking you someplace safe. We really need to go now. No arguments," the agent said. If he wasn't so cute, I might begin to think his insistence was annoying.

"Did I hear you say *we*, as in both of us? I'm supposed to go somewhere with a guy I don't know? We haven't even been on a first date yet!" Oh, boy, was that a Freudian slip!

He seemed unfazed by the unfortunate choice of words. I noticed a momentary something in his eyes, although I couldn't tell if it was amusement or interest. The agent continued like he hadn't noticed anything amiss. "If you're packed, we really need to leave immediately." He took my elbow and started for the door.

"What happened to my calm, orderly life?" I said faintly, my resistance failing. I grabbed my overnight bag and tried to keep up with his longer stride. "Are you sure this was done by the cyber thugs?" I tried to cling to the hope that my worst nightmare wasn't really happening. "Will they come back?" Staying there all alone wasn't wise, but the alternative of being forced to run and hide from these guys was even more frightening.

Once outside the apartment building, he turned to face me. "While I was on the phone, I learned a runner was picked up who'd photographed us as we left your office," he explained. "He'd started to clear the phone before he was arrested, but we got enough off it to indicate he was working with a known member of Ravens Eye Group. Now they know you've been cooperating with me. That's why they checked you out."

"So, I'm in trouble just for helping?" I said that a bit louder than I intended.

He quietly replied, "Stay calm. Don't worry, you're under my protection. I'm here to help you. I'll take you someplace where they can't get to you." He looked at me, as if deciding how to continue. "I know you've been through a lot. Sometimes it helps to get a little taste of something familiar after a bad day."

"That definitely describes the kind of day I'm having," I glumly agreed with his assessment.

"If you're hungry, we could go get something. I could really go for some Cajun food, but I'm unfamiliar with this area."

Giving it some thought, I decided to agree to his suggestion. He was just redirecting me to manage the situation, but what else could I do? "I know a place where they have the best jambalaya," I reluctantly told him.

"We shouldn't talk inside a restaurant," he said. "Is there a fast-food place nearby?"

"This place has both an eat-in area and a drive-through window," I assured him.

He nodded his head in approval and we headed for his car. "Which way do we go?" he asked.

"Just down two blocks and go right at the intersection, then left at the next light," I pointed. He gave me a sympathetic gaze, though there wasn't much else either of us could say.

At the restaurant, he listened as I started talking. I needed to unload about the object I had seen. "I originally thought the device might be an inertial positioning system, and I thought I saw some wires. I'd never seen anything like it before."

"Tell me about what that is," he said.

"Well, the surveyors use this piece of equipment in a helicopter. It lets them fly along above terrain that is physically difficult or unsafe to travel across on foot, like a marshy area or a mountain. It measures their acceleration from a control point to calculate their position and comes up with the survey measurements."

He looked at me then with surprise. "How did you come to that kind of conclusion?"

"I work for surveyors. They use the modern versions, so I've seen some. It isn't hard to put some things together."

"Let's talk more about this after we pick up our food," he suggested while he angled his car to the drive-through window and gave the attendant our order.

The food smelled delicious, and I realized that even after what had happened, I was hungry. He parked in the lot so we could talk.

"Tell me more about what you do," I asked, wanting to find out more about this nice-looking agent.

"I deal with maintaining national security," he said.

"That's pretty vague. Can you tell me anything more?" I prompted.

"My job is protecting and maintaining the security of agency assets and personnel."

"So, am I your first?" I added just to be funny. For some reason, I felt compelled to verbally spar with him a bit.

"Excuse me - first what?" He looked like he was going to swallow his tongue.

From his expression, I knew what he was thinking. "The first person you've had to protect. Have you been in this kind of situation before?" I turned toward him to see what he'd say.

He gave me a piercing gaze and said with mock seriousness, "You're not really the first, but next time I'll have to remember to ask for hazardous duty pay. As for anything else, I will neither confirm nor deny." Then the guy gave me an engaging half-smile. He knew he was being cute.

"We have the same weird sense of humor. I find that interesting. Sometimes seeing the funny side of something helps when I'm scared," I confided. I appreciated his wit. Raising my soft drink to him, I acknowledged his cleverness. We tapped our paper cups together and drank our sodas in thoughtful silence.

Eventually I had to ask, "Why are they doing this? I can't wrap my brain around it."

"Information terrorists do this because they figure they can get away with it. It's a game to see how far they can go and how much destruction they can cause. They think that with their skills, no one can stop them. No one has, yet." His green eyes showed anger for just a moment.

"What do they want with me? Since I was dragged into this, I deserve to know."

He shifted toward me as much as the steering wheel would let him. The look on his face spoke volumes. He told me, "I've seen this before. An innocent person is discredited or killed if they stumble onto Ravens Eye's activities and won't work with them. If they get to you, you'll be co-opted or dead by morning." He leaned in close to make his point, "And, in case you're wondering, they've shown they *can* get to you."

As soon as he said that I started to hyperventilate.

"Look. This isn't about you, specifically. You're nothing but a pawn to them, to be used and sacrificed at their whim. This is how they do business. I don't like to see the aftermath of what they do to innocent people." He looked down for a minute and exhaled, as if searching for how to continue. "You came to their attention by being in the wrong place at the wrong time. Now that you've been seen, they consider you a potential problem. They're uncomfortable with that. They've done things like this to others. Some of them, just for being caught cooperating with people in my line of work," the agent said sadly.

"What happens to people who work with them?" I asked.

He was quiet for a while. "A number of people only complied because they were threatened. They risked being professionally discredited, financially ruined or having their families killed." He looked discouraged for a moment. "Some of the people this group has used should have known better. In misplaced gullibility or idealism, they thought they were making a point or having fun at somebody else's expense."

He shook his head. "Then, there were those who had no conscience. They accepted the rewards Ravens Eye Group offered, with no thought about what their actions would do to other people. Ravens Eye has no morality; the consequences don't bother them. They'll ruin people and throw them away like a cheap disposable phone. So far, they've gotten away with it. That's the reason I want to go after them."

His explanation went a long way toward making me feel better. It helped to know that he had a more personal stake in this than just doing his job. Seeing his expression told me even more. I could tell that justice mattered to him, and he truly felt bad about the people who were hurt by this group. It made me wonder just what he had personally experienced, but at this point I didn't know if he would give me an answer to such a personal question.

"I begin to understand," I said into the silence. "I wouldn't like to see people I care for treated like that. I agree with you when you say you want to do something about people who terrorize others. I may not be able to do much but I feel compelled to assist. What can I do to help?" I asked him, to show I was on his side.

Agent Simeon nodded, satisfied. He rubbed the shadow of stubble on his chin. "For now, let's take one thing at a time. My people are probably tracking down the guys you identified earlier. We'll see what they know soon."

He got quiet, so I thought I'd redirect things to something more pleasant. "What is the significance of the ravens? Why did they choose that for their name?"

"There is a legend that two ravens were sent out by some powerful being to gather information and bring that knowledge back to be evaluated and used. The name is appropriate because, like the story, Ravens Eye collects data they can use to their advantage."

As that information sank in, another question occurred to me. "How is Arty connected to the gizmo? He may be annoying, but what you've suggested about him makes me uncomfortable. Could he be that greedy and treacherous?"

"Sometimes, Ravens Eye Group wants to gain an apparently insignificant piece of information or temporary access to a database. Just a minor addition here, or a deletion there, can seem harmless. Whether Arty is an unwilling pawn, or is deliberately helping them, you shouldn't let him fool you. He's very dangerous."

I paused, "That's not exactly what I was hoping to hear. What if he's being forced?"

Agent Simeon must have seen how distraught I was. He softened his tone and spread his hands in a form of silent apology. "If something can be done to help, I'll see to it. However, I'm here to protect you," he said, looking at me with honesty in his green eyes. "Look. I can get you to a secure location. This might be easier after some sleep. By the way, why don't you call me John? It looks like we're going to be together for the duration of this."

He took the leftover containers to throw them out. When he reentered the car, I quickly moved on to another question.

"What was that action you were doing at the front door of my apartment?"

"Entering like that is called 'slicing the pie' in my line of work," he said, warming to the change in conversation. I got the impression he was glad to talk about something different. He seemed happy that I was interested in his work. "It's a way to clear around corners without exposing yourself to enemy gunfire." That brief little smile of his had me mesmerized.

It became clear that a large part of John's nature was to shield the people around him, especially from a threat as big as this. I wondered what it might feel like to be protected by him. What caused that startling thought? We sat there together in the car, with the lingering smells of food and his aftershave. I forced myself to stay focused.

John pulled out from the restaurant and drove for a while in what seemed a random fashion before going to what he said was a safe place. After he got a room in an obscure motel – he insisted on doing the talking – he saw to it that I was settled in.

"What can you tell me about this technology?" I asked.

"The systems are still under development," he began. "Its Global Positioning technology was being tested. This GPS has Quantum Assisted Sensing. That will allow it to know where it is using physics, so it doesn't need satellites. Ravens Eye Group wants it because, with this system, they don't need to spend money putting satellites in orbit. They also don't have the vulnerability of being blind if the satellites are destroyed or taken off-line."

"That ability would give them an advantage and allow them to hold people hostage if the world's current satellites won't work," I stated.

John nodded. "The drone will eventually have a powerful laser onboard that can cut through almost anything to get anywhere it's programmed to go. Obstacles wouldn't be a problem. After it crashed, the GPS components were missing. We suspect it was probably crashed on purpose so Ravens Eye could get to it."

"So my guess that it was much like an inertial positioning system was fairly close. That laser attachment doesn't sound very friendly." I shuddered. "What else would these cyber thugs do with it?"

"They'll find a way to use it to their advantage. Selling it to the highest bidder lets them fund their other schemes," John said.

"It's not the kind of technology we want falling into unfriendly hands. Something like this is of greater interest to Ravens Eye Group because it could be used for leverage to politically embarrass the U.S. if it's found in an unfriendly country. That would cause a diplomatic nightmare."

"The bigger implications are frightening," I said, my mind whirling. Then I remembered something strange that Arty had said. "Arty had complained that there wasn't any other stuff in the area, but apparently he did find the GPS system."

John stopped and pondered that information. He nodded and told me, "Try and rest."

"But there's only one bed in the room. Who gets it?"

He just gave a yawn and stretched out on the couch.

"OK, Mr. Tall, Dark, and Deadly, I won't argue with that." I noticed that he smirked at the title. Shaking my head and smiling, I closed the bathroom door to change into pajamas.

He had turned out to be both frustrating and charming. His personality was starting to grow on me, but I was grateful for the little bit of space between us.

I tried to sleep in the unfamiliar bed, but had a hard time doing so. I called out to John to see if he was asleep yet.

"Yes, I'm still awake," he told me.

"Talk to me, please. I want to get my mind off of what has been going on," I asked him.

"Well, what do you want to know?" he asked.

"You could tell me a little about yourself. I just want some general conversation, please."

"Let me see. I had a pretty good childhood. My dad was in the military, so my parents and I moved around a lot. We saw a lot of the world. Travel was one of the reasons I went in the Army. Actually, it was Army Intelligence. Afterward, I got into NSA."

He sat up to look at me. "I've seen action in many places. Some of it in military service, some of it with NSA, too. It never gets any easier. Waiting for something to happen can be the worst part." He paused for a minute, and then continued, "Why don't you tell me a little about yourself?"

"You already know I work on survey data. Files and figures may not seem interesting, but the attention to detail suits me. I enjoy having the trust of the surveyors who work beside me. I know the data, and I insist on catching any discrepancies before they become problems." I figured he would think I'm boring. "The job requires accuracy and research, when necessary, to fix any inconsistencies. That may not sound exciting, I'm good at it."

"That's how you noticed some of these things going on," he surmised. "That's a useful skill." He paused for a moment. "I can't tell you how sorry I am that you've been forced into this situation. It's wrong. Stinks on ice, but there it is." His voice held compassion and the conviction of his words. "Since I told you a little about mine, why don't you tell me about your family life?"

"Well, my parents are reasonably forgiving people. Help someone see the error of their ways and go on. You know? They don't agree with holding grudges, but I just don't think they'd want me to back down from this and let others get hurt without trying to do something. Bad karma is probably the way they'd put it."

"Your parents seem like easy-going, decent people. I doubt Ravens Eye would change the way they do things, even though they know better. For now, just try to get some rest. You'll need it."

"Thanks," I said. I closed my eyes and tried to sleep. At first, nightmares kept plaguing me, then dreams of cute agents.

Morning soon came, though I didn't want to face the day after all the problems of the day before. In my tired state, I'd have accepted instant coffee, but this room didn't even have that.

Hiding out for a while and hoping it would all go away was uppermost on my mind. However, I couldn't let these thugs get the better of me. I was convinced that the best thing to do was rise to this challenge and get back into my usual routine. Grabbing some of the clothes from my hastily packed overnight bag, I got cleaned up and dressed. I came out of the bathroom, expecting to head to work.

John saw me prepared to go to my job, and shook his head. "I'd advise you to stay put."

"You want me to hide out all day in this motel room? It would look less suspicious if I kept to my routine."

John fixed me with one of his penetrating gazes that I'll never get used to. "Do you want to die?"

"Well, not really," I replied, thinking fast. "But I should at least call in and tell them I'll be on leave."

"That's not a good idea," he stated firmly.

"It's standard procedure. I'll be in trouble if I don't call," I countered.

He was unhappy, but he conceded my point. "Just don't say too much," he warned.

One of the surveyors answered the phone. I almost started telling him about my break-in, but heeded John's words.

The surveyor asked, "Have you heard the news about Arty?" Just the way he asked the question let me know it was serious.

"What happened? He's so fussy about everything, even his car." I assumed the surveyor was talking about a little scratch from a minor fender bender.

I was stunned when the surveyor blurted out the news. "We heard that Arty was in a car crash. It went over the guard rail and burst into flames. The responders said there were no survivors."

Arty was ornery, but I had never wished something like that on him. I left the surveyor with a message about my absence that day and hung up. In a wavering voice I told John, "Arty died. Do you think the thugs got him?"

"It's possible," was all he could say.

"That does it," I said. Standing up, I walked outside the nondescript little motel room and sat down by the faded front door. I stared out at the rundown parking lot for a while, trying to figure out what to do. I was rattled.

John quietly sat down beside me. His strong presence was calming. After letting me regain a little composure, he said, "I understand how you feel, but you shouldn't let anyone see you." Reluctantly, I followed him back inside the drab room.

John took a look at me, his sympathetic gaze assessing what to do next. He quietly asked, "Do you remember anything more about what Arty said, or what was said to him?"

"A guy named Sam used to talk to Arty at lunch in various places around town. I saw them a few times. I never talked to him, but he's recently visited Arty at work."

"That's probably Sam Evanston, a known technology runner for Ravens Eye Group," John stated. "He works at an engineering firm downtown."

"Arty has mentioned his name." I recalled Arty's phone conversation. "From what I overheard, it sounded like they would eventually get rid of Sam, too. Should we visit him to get some information?" I made a move toward the door, ready to leave that drab motel room.

"Hold on," John firmly said. "Don't run off like that. Remember, you need to follow procedures. So do I. I'll make a phone call."

He got no answer and left a message for Bob Smart, a man who worked with him. He looked alarmed and made a few more calls to others at NSA. He told them he couldn't reach this other agent. He sounded worried. "Keep trying to get ahold of him," he ordered.

"With all the craziness going on, why would a missed phone call be such a problem?" I asked him.

"Because he's assigned to help me, but he hasn't checked in with me or anyone else. Suddenly not answering his phone is not like him," John reluctantly said. It didn't register at the time, but that would prove to be important.

A little later, John's phone rang. When he hung up, he was perturbed. "They can't reach Smart either. No one knows where he is or why he isn't answering. I won't leave you here without protection," he added.

I looked at him, distressed by the thoughts that were going through my head. "Do you think they got to him, too? I'd like to help," I said, unsure of what that might entail.

The concern in his eyes made me even more worried. He needed to do his job, but he didn't know what to do with me. Reluctantly, he said, "I'm not thrilled with this, but there doesn't seem to be any other way till I find out what's going on." He breathed out a sigh of frustration. "Let me make a phone call to some people I can trust."

When that was done, he said, "The other agents are already on the way to Evanston's office. To save time we'll meet them there." He grabbed his long, black leather coat.

***

We arrived at Evanston's office suite, located in an upscale business park on the other side of town. A big, black government SUV pulled up behind John's red car. "There they are," he said.

A blonde woman with her hair pulled back in a severe style opened the passenger side door and got out. John went over to talk to her, and I started to follow. She glanced in my direction, but continued to talk to John.

As I came closer, John told me, "Gia, you should stay in the car till I can figure out what's going on."

"Since Evanston might have noticed me at work, do you think he might talk to me?" I mentioned it to be helpful, to the dismay of both John and the other agent. They both just shook their heads to indicate that wasn't a good idea. Taking the hint, I moved back to stand by John's car.

John finished talking to the female agent and slung his leather coat over his shoulder. He glanced my way and, with a resigned wave, called the driver over and told him to protect me.

"Are things going to get that bad?" I asked as the driver motioned that I should sit in the SUV.

The woman with John hesitated for a moment then quietly said, "My name is Smith, by the way. You never know how bad things might get."

The two moved off as John discussed the situation with her in hushed tones. She quietly asked, "What is to be done with Gia?"

"I didn't think you would appreciate being detailed to watch Gia. Smart still isn't responding. Other agents are trying to track him down. I needed to come up with something fast. At least with her here, someone I trust can keep her safe," he said, indicating the driver.

They didn't seem happy. I don't know if they realized I was reading their body language.

As the agents turned to move up the sidewalk in front of the office building, someone shot at us. John threw his leather coat over me and pushed me down on the floor of the SUV.

Fortunately, it was early afternoon and most people were busy inside the clustered buildings of the business park. The few people who were outside started looking around and running for cover.

The two agents and the driver took out their guns and looked around. John had to duck again as another shot shattered the rear windshield of a nearby car. The flying glass grazed the driver.

John and Smith fired back rapidly. The return gunfire ceased. "Stay here in the car. Can you help him?" he said firmly, motioning to the injured driver.

I nodded, too stunned to speak.

The driver pointed to the glove box and holstered his gun. I retrieved a first aid kit and got to work.

Despite my trembling hands, I got the wound cleaned. The gash on his forehead wasn't too deep. "At least you're not bleeding anymore," I told him once the bandage was in place. He indicated he'd survive.

I watched tensely as John took the lead. He bounded up the stairs two at a time, into the building. Agent Smith kept up with him as they hurried to where the shots had originated. He may be demanding at times, but I was getting to like the guy. I could relate to the personal motivations behind his actions.

When the two agents finally came back, John reached over to pull a shard of glass out of my hair. His eyes showed the extent of his worry. Once he knew I was OK, he spoke to the driver.

"Evanston's body was in the office. We must have hit the shooter because we saw some blood. The trail led to a dead end at the street on the other side of the building. We noticed tire tracks, so a car must have been waiting," John reported.

"Is this what a typical day is like for you?" I asked, still dazed from what had happened.

He just shrugged. "Pretty much."

Agent Smith nodded in agreement.

John took his coat from around me, shook off any other little bits of glass, and slung it over his shoulder.

I had to ask, "Do you figure the bad guys knew we would be here?"

John looked at me, and then pointed to a divot in the bullet-resistant window of the SUV where I had been sitting. "They knew we'd be here," John said with certainty as he holstered his gun. "It looks like they wanted to kill you, along with the rest of us." He motioned for me to follow and we went back to his car.

"What did you see in Evanston's office?" I asked John. He hesitated, so I continued. "Did you learn something that makes what I've just been through worth it?"

John thought, and recounted with precision, "Once we cleared the outer area, we advanced into the inner office. There we found Evanston's body sprawled out behind his desk. Then we briefly looked around. The file cabinets and computer have probably been cleansed of any connection to Ravens Eye Group, but our people may find something useful."

He sighed. His face looked tired and aged beyond his years. "What did Arty tell you about Evanston?"

I thought back to that encounter. "The last time I heard the name was back when Arty was on the phone and said he'd given Evanston what he'd found so far. The person on the other end wasn't happy about that. It sounded like they intended to deal with Evanston. Now, they apparently have. That's all I know."

John called other people at NSA. "The situation with Evanston has escalated. He's dead and there was a shooter who has fled. Someone from the agency will need to deal with the crime scene." He still seemed bothered. "Has anybody been able to reach Smart?"

It didn't sound like they had heard from the missing agent. At this point, I wondered if he and the recent events were connected.

Chapter 3

John scanned the area and opened the door for me to get
into his car. I sat there, numbly silent, still collecting my thoughts.
He pulled out and skillfully maneuvered through traffic. After a
while he glanced at me a time or two, but didn't ask me anything.
He's a smart guy, allowing me time to get myself together.

"What if you'd been hit, or killed?" I blurted out, once I had
calmed down a little. "You must be used to dealing with a lot of
dangerous circumstances. However, this has to be a pretty
extreme situation, and ..." I trailed off. "You really shouldn't
worry me like that," I said with emphasis.

He looked mystified at my outburst, but just kept driving.

I couldn't take it anymore. Finally, I asked him a question
I thought he might answer. "Why did you throw your coat over
me? Even at a time like this, I have to ask," I said, still a little
shaky.

In his usual direct manner, he just fingered the stiff lining
and said, "It's made with Kevlar. I wanted to make sure you were
protected." Giving me an appraising look, as if judging how to
proceed, he quietly said, "I know this is difficult to handle. One of
the worst things I've had to live with is the knowledge that, if only I
had gotten there a little bit faster, I could have stopped something
bad from happening." The sadness in his eyes indicated that he
had been through more than he was willing to tell me.

The fact that he was empathizing with me and trying, in his
own way, to relate to my feelings meant a lot to me.

What I'd just experienced stayed on my mind. "Do you
usually work with the woman who was with you? I believe she
said her name was Agent Smith."

John glanced over at me. "She's part of my operation, so
I'm familiar with her. She's good. I usually call on Agent Smart,

but with what's been going on I needed someone I knew I could trust. She's reliable and was immediately available."

I filed that information for later. To move on from the topic of the missing agent, I started trying to put this puzzling situation into perspective. "The object looked so odd to me the first time I saw it. Arty stated that he hadn't found anything else in the area. How did Will, the surveyor who left me the message, find another one?"

John turned to me and asked, "Did Arty mention anything about Will and the Quantum GPS?"

"Well, yes. Arty said I could get Will in trouble because I asked about it. Had he been talking about another unit? What do you think happened to Will? Did I cause something terrible?"

"Where is Will surveying?"

"I don't know, but I can find out back at the office," I told him.

"We need to get that information." He squealed tires as he turned the car around to head back to my workplace.

***

We went inside. It was shortly after 5 p.m. and the whole floor was quiet. The people who came to work early had already left. Only a few stragglers and the cleaning crew were around. Our footsteps echoed as we walked down the hallway to my cubicle. I threw my things on my desk and went to the file room to get the recent surveys. "Not one is the information we're after," I said, frustrated. All the fuss seemed to be about 2 North, 12 West, Seward. I turned on the computer to look up the survey number. No current ones were listed. I leaned back in my chair, still reeling from what I had been through that day.

John silently put a hand on my shoulder. When I turned to look at him, he told me, "You're doing OK." He gave an encouraging smile and went back to looking through some of the survey files. His little smile and touch made my mind go off on a tangent, till I told myself to stick to the task at hand.

Forcing myself to relax, I remembered the deletions that I'd found earlier. I looked up the township and range and found the owner's name. "This survey isn't showing up in the numerical listings, but it's showing up by township and range. It's also on the coast. Here's something interesting. It's located right next to some sort of special military testing area," I told John. "I've seen stuff on TV about Dugway Proving Ground. Could the proximity of a secure site have something to do with all these recent events?"

He raised an eyebrow, but all he would say was, "Show me what you've got."

"The look on your face tells me we're definitely on to something," I told him grimly. Taking the latitude and longitude of the survey from the map, I looked up the township and range. It was 2 North, 12 West, Seward, again. I told John, "With 23,040 acres in a township, there's too much land to just wander around in it. We need a way to find this specific survey site. Are we going to borrow some survey equipment?"

John just said, "No, I have a locator app on my phone. Give me the information and I'll plug it in." After a few phone calls to his people, he said, "Let's go." We went back to his car and headed out for the coast.

***

The way John drove, it didn't take us long to reach the area. We made it there in what must have been record time since the sun wasn't close to the horizon yet. Of course, that's not surprising in an Alaskan summer.

Once we were as close as we could get to the area in the car, John frequently checked his phone for the location and sent information to his backup. When the annoying synthetic voice said we were close, John parked his car.

John made no move to get out, but looked around from his driver's seat. After a while, three government SUVs pulled to the side of the road behind us. "There's backup," he said.

We got out and he conferred with the others. The first two vehicles carried six people. They were all getting their guns and equipment ready. The third SUV, driven by Agent Smith, held two passengers who were doing the same.

"Thanks for getting here as quickly as you could. This was short notice and I appreciate your dedication. We have to find any technology before somebody else gets to it. Let's move out," John said with authority.

John's car was left behind, and the group took two of the sturdier vehicles. They didn't seem so roomy at that point, with all the people and gear. We went down a dirt access road that led to the cut line that had been cleared around the boundary of the survey.

The computer voice indicated we were going the right way. Good thing it wasn't longer, because I couldn't have taken much more of that synthetic speech. After a while we all had to get out and walk.

"Hey, how about giving me a breather? I'm having a hard time keeping up with your long strides," I said to the two agents beside me. I was out of breath and lagging far behind the rest of the group. Those team members were obviously unhappy that I was slowing them down. I suspected they were supposed to keep watch over me because they dutifully stayed with me even though they didn't look like they needed a break

John looked back every once in a while to check on me. Finally, I motioned to him and pointed. "Over there is the site," I said, huffing and puffing. We walked over to where the surveyors had started working.

I called out and looked around, but it was eerily silent. "All the equipment is set up and still standing there, like the surveyors could come back at any time to finish their job. It isn't something they would just leave behind," I told one of the team members, but he was too busy looking around the area to pay much attention to me.

Looking around the site, I got a bad feeling. I saw a brown tarp thrown over a mound with several pairs of boots sticking out. I didn't want to inspect it too closely because I was afraid that was where the surveyors' bodies were dumped. It was a difficult thing to contemplate that Ravens Eye Group wouldn't have allowed them to live.

While John and the other team members were checking out the mound, I found a cell phone that had been dropped. I solemnly wiped the dirt off of it. In thumbing through it, I noticed that all the previously-called phone numbers had been wiped from the memory. The realization that this was probably Will's phone, and that he'd done that to protect me, made me sad.

A shot broke the sinister silence of the site. John yelled, "Get down!" while he fired back. Agent Smith and the others in the team went into action with precision. I reflexively got low to the ground to make as small a target as I could. My hands scraped across a brass cap marking one of the corners of the survey. The surveyors hadn't yet cemented this one down, apparently. I was able to pull it up easily.

That marker had obviously been hidden under the loose dirt. Beneath the brass cap was buried another Quantum GPS unit like I had seen before. Will and the other surveyors had found the one that Arty hadn't. I'll never know why, but obviously the surveyors hadn't trusted the bad guys. They had hidden it before the thugs could get their hands on it.

My co-workers had been killed instead of giving it up. Those men and women were heroes. John's attitude toward Ravens Eye Group and their tactics was understandable. It was now personal to me, too. I pocketed the trouble-making piece of electronics, along with the phone. I decided to tell somebody about it when I could.

John's team fanned out and he made his way slowly back to my side. The good guys flushed out two people. He pulled me low as a man and woman burst from the brush where they'd been hiding and started shooting. He saw I was worried and said, "Just stay down."

I nodded, but the irony wasn't lost on me as I remembered my earlier thought about not wanting to be around when it actually *was* time to panic. I quietly asked, "What should I do?"

He looked at me in astonishment. "Stay out of the line of fire so my people can do their jobs. You're not trained, and I don't want you getting in the way or getting hurt," he stated with finality.

I wanted to give him a piece of my mind for that comment, but I couldn't think of a thing to say. Besides, I wasn't going to interrupt the man when he was busy shooting at people who were trying to kill us. Telling him about what I'd found would have to wait.

John took careful aim at the woman. When she realized John was aiming at her, she tried to duck. I'll never forget that scene. As the bullet struck her, things seemed to run in slow motion, although in reality it went very fast. Little things stuck out as she crumpled to the ground. I forced myself to look away, but I'll always regret seeing the look on her face just before she died.

John eventually had to change clips. He resumed firing at the strange man, forcing him to duck for cover.

During the intervals between shots, the stranger was slowly making his way closer to us. From the nasty grin on his face, I'm sure he expected us to die.

More volleys were exchanged between John's team and the attacker. I didn't see who got him, but eventually the guy fell and didn't move again.

A rumble caught John's attention. He looked out from the survey site as the whine of motors became audible. His expression was unhappy. Clouds of dust and exhaust billowed behind a group of riders on All-Terrain Vehicles about a mile from us down the line of cleared brush the surveyors had cut for their survey.

Somehow, I didn't trust them. "Should we hide?" I asked.

John stated in his usual self-assured way, "It wouldn't do any good. They see us." He ordered, "Go. Get into one of the SUVs and lock the doors. They're armored. You'll be safer in there."

"What about you?" I asked, but he had already turned away to prepare.

Chapter 4

John tersely spoke into his mic to his people. "We've got incoming." They quickly got into position to meet the oncoming threat.

The look on his face told me this was bad, so I ran back to where the cars had been parked, as he had instructed. By then, I could see the riders approaching along the same trail we had come. I got inside and locked the doors.

In a few moments the ATVs approached the vehicle where I was hiding. As they roared by, they shot at the driver's side window and it went opaque. The bad guys thundered past to the right of the car, taking positions to attack John and his people. The radio came to life with commands being given and all the team members calling in information.

A few times, I heard people report, "Man down, man down." I had seen one team member arch backward and fall, but that verbal confirmation that he'd been shot brought stark terror to the scene. I scooted closer to the front passenger's side window to see if that had been John. Just then the window went opaque. I screamed and ducked. Peeking up at the now-cloudy window, I could see a divot from where a bullet had been stopped, inches from where my face had been!

Now I couldn't see out of either front window. I quickly crawled over the seats into the back to get a better view. It was probably just as well that I had done that when I did, because one of the gang members brought out an RPG launcher. The explosion was sensory overload as the other SUV rose up in a thundering fireball. As it crashed back down, the car I was in shuddered. It was lucky I hadn't chosen to hide in that one!

Smoke began to obscure the entire area. In the haze, I could make out red laser beams moving around, but I couldn't tell if they were from the bad guys or John's team. Someone moved through the smoke at one point, though I couldn't see who it was. Two lasers scissored together to target him and he arched backward to avoid them.   It was pretty impressive.

At one point, John announced over the radio, "Break, break. Collapse into three-man teams and return fire."   That's when more bullets began hitting the car.   I couldn't help but wonder how much punishment the armor could take.

During the shooting, the right-rear passenger window went opaque as well.   From that point on, I was unable to see what was happening.   It was terrifying and claustrophobic to be so blind. My world shrank to what I could see in the interior of the vehicle. The static-filled reports coming through the radio were my only clue to what was going on.   Some of them I could only wonder at, as I heard "Be aware - we've got dirty birds here."

All I could do was hunker down on the floor of the SUV and wait to see if someone would come knocking.   I could only hope it would be someone friendly.

Eventually, no more bullets struck the side of the car.   John came up and called my name over the radio, "Gia.   Can you hear me?   It's OK to come out now."

I opened the door and looked out onto a war zone.   I tried to stand upright, but my legs were shaking so badly I had to hang on to the door to support myself.

John came over and looked me up and down.   "Are you all right?"

I just stood there for a moment and tried to breathe.   The wind was whipping around, lashing at the trees and driving my hair into my eyes.   After a moment, I realized it was too regular and there was a quiet whirring that was gradually growing louder.   I looked up.   It was coming from helicopters, although I could see no insignia on them.

John spoke loudly so I could hear over the noise, "These guys are the reinforcements."   I hadn't heard them approach while I was in the SUV.

John went to meet the incoming helicopters.   Agent Smith came over to see how I was.   I asked her about the comment concerning the dirty birds.   She said, "That's a slang term given to the contractors hired by Ravens Eye Group.   They do the stealthy information terrorism. Any time they want to use the guns, bombs and bullets, they hire contractors to apply direct force. All of us on the team are trained in counter-terrorism tactics. Many of my team members have had to fight contractors like these guys before."

With that kind of history, it was easy to see why they came up with the derogatory term. What a nasty group. I had thought the data terrorists were bad!

The dull, black helicopters were difficult to see against the last glow of the darkening sky. There were a couple shorter, thinner ones, with projections off of "wings" from either side of the body of the craft. Then there was a larger, longer one.

When John came by I had to ask him, "Why aren't they in the usual military camouflage?" He just stated in his usual brief manner, "They're a special group with NSA."

The larger helicopter landed. A lot of armed men dressed in dark uniforms quickly got out. They had night vision goggles over their eyes.

John stood up and held his arms out from his side. Even in the twilight, the dark-clothed soldiers spotted him. As a few started toward us, he pulled me over as well, saying, "Stand still with your arms outstretched so they can see you are unarmed."

As the soldiers approached, John identified the both of us. "Most of the action is done, but we could use you on the flank. We've got contractors here." It was almost like John was speaking a different language, but they understood. He was clearly used to leadership.

"I could use some equipment," he said. They gave him a helmet with night vision goggles and a fresh rifle. He told me, "Stay put. I'm going to go with the team." With that, he left with the other men.

Not knowing what else to do, I sat back in the SUV. I could just barely make out the two thinner helicopters as they maneuvered around the remnants of the bad guys. I could see glowing arcs from time to time. Agent Smith explained to me later that those were from tracer rounds being fired from the two Apache helicopters. The other, larger helicopter was a Blackhawk.

Soon, there was nothing more coming from the thugs' location. At that point it was dark and difficult to see, but the staccato of the gunshots from John's team and from the helicopters lessened.

When John came back, he was unhappy. "They knew we'd be here. Spread out everyone. They wanted to keep us from locating that other device. We've got to find it."

People started looking around, but came up empty. The anger was clear in his eyes and I heard him swear. The helicopters were flying around and people were busy, but I could see John was frustrated. He muttered again, "It has to be here. Why can't I find it?" He's the kind of person to place more expectations on himself than on his team.

"Can I help?" That was the only thing I could think of to say. He stopped to look at me briefly. I asked, "What are you looking for?"

"They obviously expected to pick up the other Quantum device. Either there never was anything worth fighting over, or Ravens Eye has already gotten it. This might have been a delaying tactic to allow someone to get it away from here."

The look on his face told me that the situation aggravated him. Then it dawned on me. "What about this?" I asked as I gave him the unit I'd found under the brass cap.

The look on John's face was priceless. It was a jumble of disbelief and relief, and like he could kiss me and kill me all at once. However, now that John had what he needed to find, he was off to do other things.

***

The pilots of the two Apache helicopters swept the area one last time to make sure no one had evaded capture. Eventually, the air support flew off. I heard someone say they'd gotten word that the last of the thugs had been apprehended.

That news made me smile.

The fighting was through, but things weren't finished just yet. John and the other black-clad team members began to assemble by the large helicopter. Some of them had been injured.

John was dirty but unharmed. The surviving goons were brought over to him before being taken away in the larger helicopter.

When I saw Arty there among them, I was astounded. I blurted out, "I thought you were dead!"

He looked at me like I was stupid and tried to get loose, but he was tightly restrained. His anger was obvious. He cursed at John, "I wish I had gotten rid of you when I killed that worthless tech, Evanston. You're pathetic."

From where I was, I noticed that Arty was wearing a bulky bandage on his shoulder. I felt a sense of satisfaction that he was the one John had shot at Evanston's office. It felt like justice had been served that he hadn't come away unscathed.

John saw the bandage as well. "Your botched scheme didn't work as planned. I'm surprised you came here personally. You're the kind who would let contractors take the risk of finding and delivering the device. We already know that's who the extra people are."

Arty wouldn't respond to that statement.

John continued, "Any corporate or foreign power would be willing to pay a lot for the Quantum GPS technology. I'm assuming Ravens Eye offered you more than the others. Did they also agree to get you out of the country, once everyone thought you were dead?"

Arty didn't disagree. "You and the piece of office furniture you've been using don't have a clue. If I hadn't needed the money, I might have done it for free just to see you smug bureaucratic cockroaches scurry around." He laughed at his own remark. "The best you can do is to try to make sense of what we've done after the fact. We're always going to be one step ahead of you." He gave a disgruntled sigh. "This plan almost worked. All I needed was the extra time that messing with the data and faking my death should have given me. I would have been out of here, free and clear and rich enough to retire."

Arty then turned his venom on me. "And you, you little nothing. Did you like your anonymity and stability? I hope you enjoyed it while you had it, because now they know about you. I warned you your meddling would get you in trouble." He sneered, "Look what you cost your friend, Will, and the others, Gia. You have no idea what's really going on, or what's waiting for you, and you'll never see them coming till it's too late!"

That threat was chilling. I wasn't going to let Arty's snide remark get to me. After all, he couldn't do much with flex cuffs around his wrists. I kept my thoughts to myself, but I knew that he was the one who didn't know enough about the survey information to get it all deleted, which led to his plot being uncovered. I had helped in identifying some of the old surveyor's cohorts, so I knew I wasn't so insignificant!

Arty leaned in closer to John, "You may have gotten a couple contractors, but there are always more willing to take the risk for good pay." He gestured at me, "That little piece has come to count on not being noticed. She thought that would protect her. She doesn't realize that invisibility and predictability work both ways. When people see what they expect to see, they don't look any closer and they won't worry about what's going on right under their noses. When things do get bad, the sheep count on somebody else stepping in to protect them so they don't have to get involved. This isn't over yet, not by a long shot."

John replied, "Well, it's over for you. You'll have three meals and a cot to look forward to, and maybe even some outdoor time, where you're going."

Arty's betrayal shocked me on so many levels. Not only that he was more greedy and self-serving than I had ever suspected, but also that he was so uncaring about his co-workers' deaths. He had inflicted a lot of trauma on so many people. I couldn't feel sorry for him in the slightest. His statement about only seeing what is expected really hit home. That his contemptuous comment also applied to me made me feel far worse.

John turned to the guards and told them, "Get him out of here."

As the greedy old man was unceremoniously carted off, he gave us both a nasty grin.

John's face eased in relief. The technology was recovered and they had what was left of this cell rounded up.

He had achieved his victory, and I was glad. Arty's chilling words that the next time Ravens Eye Group wouldn't be stopped had me shaking. I could see why John wanted to thwart them. I resolved to do whatever I could to help.

This was the most terrifying, and the most exciting, time in my life. Despite the upheavals of the past couple of days, I almost wished for my mundane, comfortable life of blissful ignorance back again. Well, almost. Lack of knowledge is dangerous. That was a hard lesson I had learned firsthand. Yet I wouldn't give up this time with John to have my uneventful prior life back.

As they were hauling Arty and the others into the Blackhawk, I looked at John and asked, "For all the guff Arty gave me and the things he said about you, could I go over and kick him?"

John just shook his head to tell me no, but the lopsided grin and the look in his eyes said he understood how I felt.

"There are times when I'd like to do that to some of these guys, myself." My handsome agent was starting to understand my sense of humor! I could love a guy like that.

Then I asked him, "What will happen to Arty and his group, and what will you do now?"

He thought for a minute. "Arty and the remaining members of his gang should be locked up for a long time. They probably thought they'd be enjoying the sunset on a warm beach somewhere. Instead, they'll have nothing but a cold prison cell with no view." He gave a tired sigh, "As for what I'll do, there are others like him out there to find."

John motioned me toward him as a couple large black Humvees pulled up. Talking above all the noise he said, "Go with that driver," pointing at one of the vehicles. "He'll take you back to the motel to clean up and rest. Stay there. In a few days, we'll get back in touch with you." He must have seen the uneasiness in my face. "You'll need to go into protective custody. Don't worry, things will be OK."

He got serious and said, "You'd be wise to get rid of your old computer. The Ravens Eye guys are good enough to get around most antivirus and antispyware programs. Also, you'll have to 'forget' what happened here tonight. Talking about it wouldn't be a good thing."

I nodded in understanding. "No one would believe me if I tried to tell them, anyway."

He leaned over to me and gave me a quick hug. He said in my ear, "Thank you for your help."

Blushing, I brazenly toyed with the idea of perhaps leaning in to give him a kiss, but just at that point he released me. "I'm grateful I could help," I replied. I've received less-than-genuine thanks before, but the look in his eyes held sincerity. I hoped they also held something more. "Shouldn't people know about what the bad guys are doing and the threat they pose? I know I can't say anything, but how are people going to be protected from them?"

John smiled at me and chuckled, "Be careful about donning a superhero cape." He got thoughtful after that and said, "About all the average person can do is be smart, be alert, and take precautions. Today's accomplishment is a good start. It'll slow them down, but it won't stop their organization." He turned to leave, then looked back at me and said, "I need to go with the others covering Arty and his group."

That was his way of saying goodbye. I just couldn't let things end like that. I blurted out, "Wait!" He turned back to me, but I couldn't think of anything more to say. After all, what else was there? Thinking quickly, I exclaimed, "Would you let me go with you in the helicopter?"

He just smiled that usual little half-smile of his. There was a momentary hesitation. I saw something I couldn't define shine briefly in his eyes. My heart sped up as I anticipated that he might actually allow my request. He put his hands on my shoulders and shook his head saying, "Where I'm going, you don't want to go."

"Why do you always have to be so mysterious?" I pretended to grouse a little, just to tease him. I smiled at him then and said, "I understand." With mock sternness I told him, "You'd better take care of yourself."

His mouth twitched in a little grin and his eyes crinkled. He seemed relieved. "Will do. You take care of yourself, too." He turned to rejoin the others.

I watched as some of the NSA people clamored to talk to him. He spoke to them in low, serious tones.

***

The driver got out of the Humvee and cleared his throat.   I turned around and prepared to go back to the city.

As we set out, I opened the window a little and let the wind blow on my face to dry the moisture forming in my eyes.   So many emotions were fighting to come to the surface.   I sighed.

The driver cast a worried look at me.

I smiled and said, "So much has happened.   It's difficult to believe that my life will ever be the same again," and returned to my thoughts.

The driver nodded and left me alone.

I was filled with sadness for all the death and destruction. Despite it all, there was still a glimmer of hope.   Would these good guys be successful?   Would John and I get together?

In the end, there was only one further question: Where had John gotten that cool leather coat?

Chapter 5

Recent events had taught me the hard lesson that it's easier to ask the question than it is to find the answer. Living with the consequences of gaining that knowledge is an altogether different and difficult thing to manage. There was more going on around me than I had originally known, and people weren't always what they seemed.

Ravens Eye Group now knew about me, so I was going to be relocated for my protection. Safety was good, but it unfortunately meant I had to move out of state. The program relocated me to a little community outside of Seattle, Washington.

When I groused and asked "How long will this be?" John told me, "It might be a month or more until you need to testify to the grand jury." I was given a job in a nondescript governmental office in an undisclosed (and equally nondescript) area, far from anyone who knew me.

On the bright side, I told myself that maybe a change of scene would clear my head and I could start fresh. I didn't relish the necessity of packing and moving, but fulfilling one's civic duty isn't always pleasant.

Leaving my old job with the surveyors was something I did with mixed feelings. Hiding meant giving up a lot of things. It constantly bothered me that Arty, a trusted co-worker, could be so corrupt and contemptuous of other people's lives. I didn't want to contemplate how many other deaths he may have caused. It shook my faith in humanity to the core.

John wasn't able to divulge if there might be others having to stay in protection as well, or if I would get to meet them. I worried if there were other groups similar to Arty's and what they might be doing.

All he would say was, "You know I can't answer that."

"What questions will this grand jury ask me?"

He spread his hands and said, "That's up to them." The lack of information, while familiar, began to be aggravating.

"Would you be able to visit me occasionally?" His calming presence in this storm of change was something I craved.

He just cryptically answered, "When I can. You need to lie low. That's why you're being relocated to an obscure job. You could take this time to learn whatever is online, to keep occupied. You could pick up some blending lessons," he said helpfully.

"I'm already pretty proficient at being overlooked at work; however, I see your point about staying busy."

His remarks were probably supposed to assuage my growing worries, but I was left with more questions than answers. After two weeks' notice at my previous job, and a lot of preparation for my move, I finally headed out to my new destination. All I could do was hope that I was up for whatever this new and unknown job would entail.

On the way to my new duty station, I tried out my phone's mapping-and-directions app. It isn't as easy as they make it seem. I got sidetracked a few times when I gave it the wrong input. That cost me some time. Everything was unfamiliar. By the time I was on the highway I needed to take, it was early afternoon.

I decided that the next off-ramp was the perfect place to get a bite to eat and a nap. I gratefully pulled in to the very end of the rest stop. It was quiet and mostly empty. I would be protected in the deep shadows. The trees were bigger than what I'd been used to up north. My car wasn't visible from the front end of the parking lot, so I had a private shady area to doze.

John's people had impressed on me the need to be careful. It never occurred to me that a rest stop could put me in such danger. I adjusted my seat and the afternoon warmth lulled me into a false sense of safety.

A while later, something woke me. As I looked around, still fuzzy from my nap, I began to notice that the wind had picked up a lot. The branches of the trees protecting my car were whipping around. The leaves and evergreen needles were being blown everywhere. I assumed it meant a storm was moving in. I had only been asleep for a couple hours, but the mid-afternoon sun cast a dazzling pattern across my eyes through the wildly moving tree limbs.

Then I sat upright and saw it. It was a stubby aircraft, matte black with orange blotches and big engines that were now tilted downward as it was landing. This unmanned aerial vehicle was remotely piloted. It was larger than the small drone we'd found before. It looked bigger than one of those Global Hawk drones. The attachments hanging from the wings of the aircraft were like the weapons struts attached to the sides of the helicopters I remembered seeing. That was obviously the purpose here, but these were empty.

Holding the phone up, I hit record and watched the screen. Lying back in the seat, I hoped no one could see something as small as a cell phone through the tinted window.

This was another strange incident. Asking questions had gotten me right in the center of Ravens Eye's crosshairs in the first place. I recalled the terrifyingly brutal things I had learned about the cyber thugs. John had made it clear what might happen to me if I was caught.

The large vehicle just landed and sat there for a while. As if on cue, a car approached and parked. The operator immediately got out of the vehicle. He was wearing a military uniform and had a piece of electronics with a joystick, not too far different from one of those game devices.

I adjusted the phone and did my best to watch the screen and angle around tree branches. The operator was focused on his activity and didn't pay attention to anything else till another car drove up. Two big guys got out and drew weapons. Next, I heard some yelling, a pop, and a thud. My eyes were glued to the screen as the phone captured the execution of the drone operator. It wasn't pretty.

Gasping for breath, I felt like maybe I wanted to throw up, or run away, or scream, but I had to stay hidden. I hoped I remained unnoticed in the afternoon shadows. The thugs started dealing with the corpse, piling it into the car like picking up so much trash.

As I watched, someone dressed in a lab coat got out of the other car. He casually walked around the puddle of blood like he was used to seeing such gore. The replacement pilot worked the joystick. The engines came to life in another whoosh of wind and noise.

I kept recording as the UAV zoomed off straight up and went out of sight, with the thugs following it. It was chilling to think what Ravens Eye would do with something like a Quantum GPS unit. Contemplating the added capability of a UAV as big as this one, equipped with weapons and vertical take-off and landing, made me come to the conclusion that this was a nightmare scenario.

I stayed reclined and hidden till I couldn't hear their vehicles anymore. While waiting, I sent the video I'd taken of the men and the UAV to John, and gave him what information I could. While I wanted to see what he might say, I knew he would be unhappy with me. After all, I wasn't supposed to be snooping on the bad guys!

Eventually, it was safe to leave, and I began to adjust my seat. Considering the odd occurrence, getting much further away was probably the better thing to do.

I pulled the car out to get back on the highway, but was blocked by a couple black SUVs. I smiled as I hoped that might be John.

A taller man with a receding hairline swaggered over to my car. His bravado was at odds with his paunch and the sweat on his brow. That's definitely not John, I thought. I was disappointed. The man looked at me while taking a moment to wipe his forehead, and rapped on my window, indicating he wanted me to roll it down.

From the second SUV stepped a shorter, darker man who started to walk over to my vehicle.

The man with the thinning hair called to him, "I'll get this contained."

The shorter agent nodded and walked back to his car. He leaned against the door, watching.

Reluctantly, I pressed the button to retract the window and said, "What's going on?"

"What are you doing here?" the taller man asked, not trying to be polite.

"I just stopped off to drink some coffee from my thermos," I told him, trying to hold my irritability in check. It was the truth, just not all of it. I felt uncomfortable with giving these strangers any more information than was necessary.

"Where are you headed?" he asked rather abruptly.

"Um, I was just heading back to the highway." Something about this whole situation set my nerves on edge. It was altogether too much of a coincidence for these two to show up right after what I had witnessed. It was too convenient. I certainly wasn't going to tell these unfamiliar guys the undisclosed location where I was supposed to go, or the crime I had just seen. The only plan I could think of was to turn the questioning back on him. "Who are you?"

"I'm an agent, just like Simeon." he said, his eyes glancing suspiciously around the area.

The other agent joined him.

I was a little cautious and said in a dubious tone, "Really? What agency are you two with, and how do you know, uh, Agent Simeon?" I stumbled over his name, because I had gotten used to calling him John, but didn't want to do that in front of these strange men.

They were taken aback by my question. "We're aware he's been working with you," the taller and older man said.

"He's on another case. We've both partnered with him on occasion," the shorter agent said, smiling like he thought that would gain my trust.

Thinking fast, I responded, "Well, if you know him, you know he would instruct me not to trust anyone who didn't identify himself to me." I hoped that would stall them.

The shorter agent showed me some convincing I.D., but the taller one was reluctant. "I've told you all you need to know," he insisted till I crossed my arms and gave him a challenging look. He finally relented. According to the I.D., the taller agent was Bob Smart. That was a familiar name. John had mentioned working with him.

"Have you and Agent Smart been working together very long?" I said, turning to the shorter agent. I just wanted to see what the man's answer might be.

"Not long," he tersely replied. This was curious, because the last I'd heard, Smart was supposed to be partnered with John.

Partners could be moved around from time to time, I surmised, but it heightened my wariness.

"Did you see or hear anything odd?" Smart interrupted the conversation, adamant to find out what I might know.

I decided to be careful and edit what I told them. "Like I told you, I drank some coffee, and then I decided to leave. You saw me start pulling out when you drove up." That was true. To make my point, I feigned innocence and asked them, "Why? Did something interesting happen? It's obvious that you two are in the middle of investigating something."

"So you're telling us you never noticed anything out of the ordinary? You didn't even see the puddle over there?" Smart asked me, without answering my questions. He was getting irritated and was as distrustful of me as I was of him.

I sighed to indicate my growing frustration. Emphasizing each word, I repeated, "Like I said, I drank some coffee. And, yes, I tried to avoid driving in the ketchup, or whatever that might be." I looked him in the eye to show my truthfulness about those words. "But I can tell John, uh, Agent Simeon that you're interested in whatever might have occurred here. I'm sure he could help." To make the point that I'd be willing to call John into this, I reached for my phone.

My heart was pounding, and my gut was telling me to get away from them. Hoping I wouldn't have to go through with it, I started to dial.

Both agents gave me that look John usually wears the more I get involved. It was obvious these strangers viewed me as a loose end, but hopefully I'd been more frustrating than they wanted to handle and would let me leave.

Eying each other quickly, Smart said, "We don't want you in the middle of our investigation, so head on out of here and let us get to work." They motioned me to go, telling me, "Don't bother Agent Simeon. We can handle things here." They didn't like the idea of getting John involved. That confirmed my suspicion. "Go on your way," Smart said dismissively, as I pondered their peculiar attitude. He still eyed me with blatant doubt.

"OK. I understand." I put the phone down and prepared to drive off. I knew I'd better not push things further. It was safer to leave immediately, since I didn't want to antagonize them. They weren't going to give any additional information.

The two agents walked back to their cars, still giving me suspicious looks. Before I punched the button to raise the window again I heard the shorter agent tell Smart, "If she starts nosing around she'll cause trouble." Smart's reply was lost when I started my car, but I noted that he gave a smirk that sent chills down my spine.

Heading out, I gave them a jaunty wave, but the situation nagged at me. Unanswered questions bother me. Besides, it wasn't my fault that I was dragged into the middle of this. I thought about what I'd captured on my phone and wondered about Smart and his friend. Something about them felt off, like they were involved somehow. Or were they just unhappy that I wasn't "one of them"?

Back on the highway I did the speed limit, but it didn't take long before two familiar black SUVs raced past me. At the speed those two agents were going, I doubt they noticed me.

If those guys have left, who's controlling the scene at the rest stop? After all, that's what they do in the crime shows. Faced with that unanswered question, I decided to return and see what was going on firsthand. That, at least, would tell me something vital. It could be that some other agents had taken over securing the area. Somehow, I just didn't think so.

At the next off-ramp, I made my way back. I slowed down before the turnoff to the rest stop to see if anyone was there. The area was totally vacant, and there were no agents protecting the scene. As I pulled in I noticed that there wasn't even some yellow tape to indicate the site was being investigated. The only indication that someone else had been there was some cola had been poured onto the pavement where the blood had been. Another bit of crime show trivia I have picked up is they often use cola to dissolve blood stains.

The parking area had been made to look like nothing had ever happened. Finding out the investigation wasn't real made me angry. I cursed and hit the steering wheel. At least it helped to get the fear and anger out of my system. I immediately called John and asked, "Shouldn't there be some action on this? Why isn't this crime scene being protected?"

John was taken aback about the two agents and their actions, but confirmed that they were known to him. He told me, "I'll note it for further investigation. These things take time, and there must be proof before accusations can be made. Everyone deserves due process. If something is going on, we don't want to tip our hand."

"I was hoping for a more direct response, but I understand the workings of bureaucracy."

John confirmed my suspicions when he told me, "That craft you unfortunately saw was stolen. As for the shooting, I'm sorry you had to witness that, but weren't you told not to get involved?"

"I was only stopping off for some coffee and decided to take a nap. I wasn't trying to get involved in anything," I said a bit defensively. However, the topic of the craft that I wasn't supposed to have seen brought up some questions.

"The tilting engines on that UAV were unusual. The matte black coloring was vaguely like that other drone we found, though this one was bigger. It looked like various weapons could be put on those struts. And what's with the orange blotches on the skin, anyway?"

At the description of the vehicle, he hesitated. "It's a new type of UCAV; an unmanned combat aerial vehicle. The orange blotches signify either a training craft or an experimental one. The matte black skin blocks radar detection." He cautioned me, "Those aren't pieces of information to spread around."

My mind raced when I took what I'd just learned and added it to what I'd seen. "Well, shooting the original operator to steal the UCAV might be one thing, but doesn't it have some sort of GPS to track it? And what about those two agents who said they know you. Do you think Ravens Eye Group is involved?"

John answered in a serious tone, "That prototype was being tested. The geo-positioning instrumentation was removed." He was quiet for a moment and said, "The involvement of Ravens Eye Group remains to be seen. Thanks for the videos you sent and the information about the two agents. I'll check it out."

"What would Ravens Eye want with such a large craft?   Is there a connection with the Quantum GPS?"

"Don't worry, I'll check it out," John repeated.   "It's better for you to get out of there and get back on the road.   Be careful.   If these people are willing to kill an operator and steal a UAV, they aren't messing around."

I took his advice and headed out quickly, keeping a lookout for any black SUVs.

***

In the early evening, I pulled into a little motel and got a room.   Once settled in for the night, I tried to sleep, but thoughts of GPS units and wing struts waiting for missiles made me toss and turn for a while.   Where could an aircraft that size be hidden?

Finally, I took out the phone book and looked up airplane mechanic shops in the area.   A couple aircraft shops were located near-by.   One was "Aero-Parts," and they only worked on small civilian aircraft.   That business was probably not very interesting to the thieves.   The other place was "Rich's Mech-Air," which seemed to work on almost anything that could fly.   That one was the more promising of the two, so I wrote down the information.

The similarities between this encounter and the previous one with Arty and the Quantum GPS unit piqued my curiosity.   I couldn't let this go.   Besides, the threatening manner of the two agents disturbed me.

I decided to get an early start in the morning and just take a quick look at this Mech-Air shop.   Surely that wouldn't do any harm.   If I saw anything interesting, I could tell John and be on my way.   That was all the justification I needed.

Chapter 6

Early the next morning, I checked out. As I prepared to get on the road, I debated whether to get breakfast and some coffee before seeing the shop area, or after. If in doubt, get coffee first!

The "Mech-Air" shop was just a little off the route to my destination. I wouldn't lose much time. More than just satisfying my curiosity, it would assist John, I reasoned. The road to trouble is paved with good intentions.

When I reached the place, there were no cars in front, so I pulled behind the shop. There were two big black vehicles parked in back. With a feeling of unease, I recognized them as the ones from the rest stop. Behind the SUVs was a run-down hangar. Beyond that building ran an old, private runway. It had seen better days, but a craft that could land vertically wouldn't require a new, smooth landing strip.

The hangar was old and not very big, but it could still house the drone I'd seen. The place looked promising, and those familiar vehicles led me to do further investigation. I parked my car off the main road a little ways up from the cutoff to the shop. It would look less suspicious that way. I didn't like the thought of those two agents catching me.

Leaving my car back on the road, I cut through the trees and bushes along the side of the business entrance. I prided myself on being clever enough to keep from being seen.

Getting to the hangar behind the office building wasn't as easy, since there were no trees to hide me. A side door was opened just enough to peek in. No one was in view, so I thrust my phone in to see the interior. Some men further inside were complaining about all they were expected to do to earn their pay. John could use the information, so I zoomed in to record everything. I quickly pulled the phone back outside.

Checking the pictures, a familiar black-and-orange UAV was clearly being dismantled. I captured the images of the two men who were working in the hangar. My adrenaline was pumping as the faces of the two agents who had questioned me at the rest stop also showed up in the photos.

I listened as the two agents talked with the workers. "When you two are done crating the parts, deliver them to the air show. They'll be loaded on the plane from there." I sent the pictures and information to John, along with a quick text not to trust those two agents.

As I eavesdropped, I remembered that there is a location feature for tracking cell phones. I sent another message to John: "I'll put my phone inside one of the boxes so they can be followed as they are taken from the 'Mech-Air' shop to the air show."

The conversation from the hangar quieted. No one seemed to be moving around, so I slowly opened the door again and crept inside. As my eyes adjusted to the dim light, I saw some boxes labeled farm equipment. Large sections would make it quicker to reassemble. I sent a picture of the boxes to John as well.

Edging back toward the door I had entered earlier, I was horrified to see it was now opening! Ducking behind some equipment to hide, I tried to be very quiet. The two workers got closer. If I tried to make a run for the hangar door, they'd see me. They talked about later shipping the UCAV to a foreign country, depending upon who bid the most money.

John sent me a message just then. It was a good thing I had turned the notification sounds off, because the two guys I was hiding from were close enough to have heard them. John texted, "I have the information you sent, now get out of there." I wanted to, believe me! His response was puzzling because I had expected him to come get the bad guys and pick up the drone. At the time, I hadn't stopped to think about what I'd gotten myself into and whether it was something I couldn't handle.

The two workers concentrated on dismantling the craft. With the noise they were making, I opted to make a desperate text to John, "I'm stuck where I am. I need you." After a while John finally replied, saying, "I'm a little busy." I knew that wasn't a good thing.

One of the two workers decided to head to the other end of the building. The other one walked over to the far side of the hangar to smoke. Once they were out of sight, I slipped my phone into one of the "farm equipment" boxes and headed quietly outside.

Back in my car, I calmed down and thought about the situation. First on my list of things to do is to replace my phone, I enumerated to myself. Make that the second thing. The first is to quickly head out of here, preferably without being seen by the two agents again. Things were getting complicated, and it looked like I would be arriving in Seattle a little later than I'd planned.

At the next town I came to, I stopped and purchased a cheap throwaway phone. By the time I'd had lunch and the purchase and activation of the phone was done, I figured the crates should be moving. My plan was to follow from a safe distance and avoid danger.

Before I headed out I sent people an update of my new phone number. I told them that I had stopped for lunch and I was back on the road. "Traffic is running slow right now. There might be an accident up ahead, but I'll be there as soon as I can," I reassured them.

I decided not to tell them that what I was actually doing was now tracking and tailing some bogus farm equipment, since I didn't know who I could trust at this point.

Back on the interstate, I stayed alert for any semis that might be carrying the stolen drone parts. It never occurred to me they would use long-bed pickups till some sped by me heading down the highway. When I noticed that both vehicles were loaded with large containers of farm equipment, I tailed them.

To keep the drivers from recognizing that they were being followed, I took the next exit, figuring I could wait a little bit and then get back on the highway to avoid notice. One of the trucks decided to take that exit, too.

"Play it cool. You don't want to give yourself away," I muttered to myself.

I continued till I could pull into a motel parking lot. It was early evening by then, and I was planning to stop soon, anyway. When the truck pulled in to the same parking lot, I got worried. I fervently hoped that I hadn't been discovered.

The guys from the truck just went inside and didn't pay any attention to me. When they moved off, I went over to look into the truck bed. In the back were the same boxes I'd seen at the shop. Something told me it was a better idea not to hang around.

I texted John the situation, telling him about the new phone and the license plate of the truck. I could only hope it would be helpful, but I got no response back.

The unexpected purchase of another phone used most of my available funds. That meant getting a motel room wasn't in the budget. Reluctantly, I drove down the road and parked in a vacant lot just far enough away from the motel so the two guys wouldn't see my car. I turned off the engine and reclined the seat to try to sleep, but I couldn't relax. "John still hasn't responded. Darn! That man is always making me worry!" I said after checking the phone yet again.

Bright headlights came and went in a random pattern. Even though I was troubled about what might have happened to John, the noise of passing cars soon lulled me into a fitful sleep.

***

The weak dawn light and the noise of increasing traffic insinuated themselves into my consciousness the next morning. I had to take a moment to collect myself after a restless night. I promised myself never to do that again as I worked a knot out of my neck. "Note to self; car seats don't make good beds!" John still wasn't responding, which added to my irritation.

It was early, so I got some coffee and breakfast at a nearby fast food place. Passing by the motel to head back to the Interstate, I noticed that the truck with the stolen parts was already gone. I was glad that those trucks could be tracked without being obvious.

After a boring number of hours on the highway, where I occasionally stopped and texted John to keep him updated, the trucks pulled off the highway in to an airport. I saw the signs about events happening at the airshow. This must be the place Bob Smart had mentioned.

My car went unnoticed as I followed the trucks through all the traffic and confusion. I blended into the crowds waiting to pay their admission and park. Once I found a spot, I kept John posted that the trucks were at the air show.

Keeping up the pretense of traffic, I also texted those who were expecting me that there was slow-going traffic up ahead (which was true, getting into the airport). They wanted to have regular updates on my progress, but I didn't know who I should trust or how much was necessary to tell them. This was supposed to have been a short and straight-forward drive to the confidential location. The trip shouldn't have required a lot of security, but it had turned into something quite different.

I joined the crowds and watched as the pickups seemed to converge at one of the huge cargo planes on display. That was how they planned to move the parts. Masking their activity among the busy airport displays and the people milling around the aircraft exhibits was certainly a clever ploy.

I read an interesting bit of information on a sign describing the cargo plane that was the focus of all the pickup trucks. This type of plane doesn't need a long runway. Maybe there are no long landing strips where they're taking the parts.

I sent John a text to tell him what I had found out about the plane. I got a response that his phone was out of service. It could be broken, or he could be too far from a cell tower. No matter how I tried to reassure myself, it was unbearable to think that he might have been hurt or killed. Nevertheless, I felt that he might need this information, so I walked over to the tower. Inside, in what was still the public part of the building, I asked how I could find where the cargo plane was going.

The person behind the desk said the flight plans were on the touch screen terminals on the opposite wall. "I have the aircraft number already, so it shouldn't be too hard to find," I said to the person gratefully. At the first available computer, I typed in the data. Eventually the information was displayed. I eagerly read that this cargo plane was scheduled to fly to a small private airport outside Moscow, Idaho. The plane's ability to land on a short runway would make sense there.

If I left immediately, I might just make it there before the plane was scheduled to land. Taking this step without John was worrisome. Pondering the consequences made me hesitate. If I read the flight plan correctly, they weren't going to take off till the next morning, anyway. That was undoubtedly to give the trucks and people time to filter through the hustle and bustle of the air show without drawing too much attention. If I could beat them there, it might help John. That made up my mind.

Just as I was leaving the building, I bumped into two guys who looked very familiar. It was the two I had seen back at the hangar, and again at the motel!

At first, I tried to be nonchalant. When I tried to go around them and just continue on my way, they continued watching me with suspicion.

It was time to turn the suspicion from myself onto them. As they glared at me, I turned to face them. With a big, brassy smile, I asked them, "Say, you look familiar. Do you two good looking guys go to the Rack-em and Stack-em Bar? I'm pretty sure I've seen you there!"

They just hurried away. I had to chuckle because I was certain I heard one of those bruisers tell the other guy, "One of these days you're going to get me in trouble."

Trying not to attract any further attention, I made it through the crowded air show. Returning to my car, I got back on the highway. Fortunately, I started making good time on the interstate to Idaho.

Once I hit the state border, I pulled off and was using my new phone's map function for directions. As I figured out the route to reach the airport, I also pondered why they were stopping in Moscow, Idaho. Why weren't the thieves going straight to their foreign buyers? This stop might be to hide their true destination or allow more time for bidding. Questions like that wind up getting me in trouble.

The airport surprised me. It was such a tiny place. What would they plan on doing at an unused runway? However, landing on a shorter runway at an unfrequented place with no witnesses would be to their advantage.

Away from the little control tower was a gas station, much like one where I would fill my car's tank, only this had aviation fuel. There was also an outlying building beyond the gas station. I hid my vehicle on the far side of that one so it wouldn't be seen.

I got out and wandered back to the main building. Nothing was going on, so I went back to my car to sleep. "Lovely. It's going to be another cramped night where I get to do nothing but toss and turn." I sincerely hoped that the back seat would be better, but it wasn't. "One night isn't fun. Two nights of this is definitely getting old."

***

Early the next morning, the hum of engines drew me from my car. The plane from the airshow angled in for a landing. The wingspan was too large to use the refueling area a small private plane would use, so a truck pulled up to refuel it. I ducked into the gas station to keep from being seen. Hidden inside the building, I stealthily watched their activities. A few dangerous-looking men with guns patrolled around the plane while it was being refueled. Some dealt with the back of the plane once it was lowered.

I took as many videos of the men as I dared and sent them off to John to help him apprehend as many of these guys as possible. By that point, he still hadn't replied. "You'd better not be ignoring me, and you'd better not be dead," I fretted.

Since the bad guys were refueling the plane, they were probably planning on flying to some foreign country next. Taking off from a little out-of-the-way place might be less obvious. No flight plans would mean there would be no documentation of their journey. They were covering their tracks.

Some of the men immediately headed into the gas station. They probably wanted to do a quick check to make sure they had no witnesses. The nearest hiding place was the ladies' room. I took a chance, since no guy would go in there. Lame, I know, but you'd be surprised what works.

Someone did open the door, but I had hidden in one of the stalls by crouching on the toilet seat so they couldn't see my feet underneath the partition or my head above the stall. My heartrate sped up as I heard footsteps across the tiled floor. Someone was walking into the room to check it out. Trying to keep my breathing quiet while keeping the door of the stall closed enough so I wouldn't be seen wasn't easy. I hoped the person wouldn't come any closer.

Soon, I heard a muttered, "I don't get paid for this." The footsteps receded across the floor and the door closed. I breathed a sigh of relief. It was fortunate that this room had a window so I could peek outside. Once the window was opened, I was able to quietly turn a trash bin over and climb out.

Dropping down to the pavement outside the building, I crouched in the shadows. I watched the activity going on around the plane, and pondered John's silence. That bothered me. No matter how I worked things around in my mind, I still didn't know what to do.

Unfortunately, with the preparations done, the men started heading back to the plane. A couple other guys came around the corner of the building and spotted me. They were armed, so there was no sense putting up a fight. I felt totally foolish for not having waited a little longer.

They forced me into the cargo hold and tied one of my hands to a strap using a flexi cuff. Looking around, I saw that the crates were labeled as farm equipment. They were securely tied down, though the straps were worn. This was a bad situation. However, I remembered John's commitment to stop these guys. That thought gave me courage.

One of the four workers was just about to check my pockets when we heard clanking. I looked over as another two people came up the ramp to the area where I was held captive. This hold was getting crowded. The underlings all stopped and paid attention to the newcomers.

One man had an unfamiliar accent. He said, "Well done in getting the acquired merchandise this far. You will see your first twenty-million-dollar installment credited to your offshore account within the hour. When the UCAV is delivered, an additional twenty million dollars will be deposited. Once the craft is fully reassembled, it will be tested to confirm its capabilities. That is just to be sure no important parts have been left out. If it passes, you will then receive the third payment of twenty million."

I tried not to gasp at the magnitude of the cost.

The foreign-sounding man came around some of the boxes, and looked right at me. It was the same suave-looking information broker shown being arrested on the newscast John and I had seen. He walked with an aura of command. His tailored clothes showed he had the money he'd been discussing.

One of the guards asked if he should shoot me immediately. "That would be reckless," the well-dressed man said with authority. "We cannot leave anything to tie us to this place, and we do not want any officials snooping around. Besides, do you know how hard it is to get blood out of this fabric?"

The guard looked unhappy, but the stylish man continued, "There is no time. We need to leave now. We can deal with her later." This guy was the leader. He took my jaw in his hand and looked me over. He wasn't being rough, but his look was serious. I didn't know if I should be scared, or if I should spit in his face.

Chapter 7

My eyes bugged out, I'm sure, as I wondered whether or not I should antagonize this dangerous man. I cast my eyes downward and didn't look directly at him.

He tightened his grip slightly and forced me to look in his eyes as he took a close assessment of me. It was almost like he was trying to tell me something, or he was expecting to see a certain reaction. Apparently he didn't see it or I didn't get whatever it was he was trying to impart.

After this inspection of me and the conversation with the others ended, the workers dealt with the ramp. That left me all alone in the cargo area. The doors to the hold shut with an ominous sound. "Now how am I going to get out of here?" I said frantically. There was only a little window nearby, but not much could be seen.

With no other options, I sat there and tried to phone John with one hand tied. There was still no answer, so I texted him that I was stuck in the plane. This time I actually got a phone call. I checked the number, but it wasn't from anyone I knew. I couldn't be in worse trouble, so I answered it anyway.

"John! It's actually you!" I said as the plane's engines began to whine. "I've called and texted you! I've got a lot to tell you, and it looks like we're about to take off," I began.

He interrupted me to say, "My phone was damaged. I'm just borrowing another one. This will have to be quick. Tell me what's going on." Gunfire punctuated his conversation.

I filled him in, "I followed the parts to the airshow and found the plane. Next, I drove to this little Idaho airport to see what they were doing. Now I'm stuck on the plane. The guy who was in the news being arrested for data theft seems to be paying the bad guys for the robbery and they're about to take off…"

"Wait, you're about to take off?" he interjected. "You're killing me! Why would you... how did you... Never mind." He sighed, "You're probably about to lose signal, so you'll be on your own till we get there. Don't worry, we're on our way. I can't see an alternative to this position you're in. Just stay calm and don't do anything rash. Can you hide?"

"My hand is tied, so no hiding," I said, my hope sinking.

"Don't tell them anything. They could dump you out of the plane if you anger them or if you give them any reason to think you don't have any information they want." His voice faded and was lost as the plane roared down the little runway and took off, with me inside it.

"Say nothing and don't antagonize them. Are you actually implying that I'm deliberately going to irritate them?" The silent phone didn't appreciate my sarcasm, though. In my anger and fear, I actually began to envision painful things that I could inflict on him. "How about some thanks for trying to help you?" I huffed before I dumped the poor, mute phone back in my pocket. After a while, I cooled down enough to reason things through. "He has experience and I don't." While I could understand his annoyance and frustration, it wasn't much comfort.

Soon the plane began veering and maneuvering violently. From my vantage point I couldn't see much, but it sounded like a couple jets were after us. Their wakes buffeted the slower cargo plane again and again. From the short length of time we'd been in the air, we were probably still in U.S. airspace. I surmised they were U.S. military jets.

A jet roared by us again. The cargo plane became much too unsteady for me to lean over to the window. It was an unhappy thought that the pilots might actually shoot us down or keep doing this and force us to crash. What could I do in this situation? That was something to think about besides impending death.

The erratic shifting continued. A few straps loosened and some crates began sliding. It didn't take long before the plane's haphazard movement caused the entire cargo to shift and the plane began to roll.

The load had moved so forcefully that I began to worry if the cargo straps would hold. A few times, I was sure I was going to be flattened, and I was slammed around painfully. At that point, one of the guards came back to see what was happening with the crates.

Just then, a jet thundered by and the plane lurched and dove, sending everything shifting once more. The ties failed and I had to move aside.

The bad guy was crushed between two containers as they slammed together. I shut my eyes to block the view, but I couldn't muffle the gruesome gurgle as he died. "Hopefully, it was quick," I implored whatever benevolence the universe may possess. I could almost feel sorry for him.

The fastening that held my wrist snapped as well. Finally, I was freed. The welt where it broke stung, but I was otherwise all right. I began to wish for a parachute. OK, not that I'd know how to use one! I actually pondered taking an online federal parachute training course, if they offer one.

Yelling from the cockpit area made me think maybe they had decided they'd had enough and had opted to land as quickly as they could. Things quieted down and the ride got smoother as the plane descended.

Taking advantage of the calm, I made my way to the body and checked for a pulse, but there was nothing I could do. He was definitely dead. I figured I might as well take his gun. It could come in handy. His holster was just reachable, so I delicately took the pistol with two fingers and dumped it in my pocket. Not the most pleasant experience, I can tell you!

***

The plane bumped to a stop on a little one-runway landing strip in the desert. It looked like something only desperate, lawless people would use.

Once the plane stopped, I began to think about how I was going to get out of the hold. Through the little window, all I could see was uninviting scrub. I had no idea which way I should go. Crates had shifted haphazardly all over the place, so if there had been a way to open the cargo hatch from the inside, I couldn't have gotten to it. I waited behind one of the battered crates, ready to run down the ramp as soon as the hold was opened.

At one point, someone came back, probably looking for their unfortunate comrade. They weren't able to get very far into the hold. I stayed hidden and quiet, but I kept my unsteady hand close to the pilfered gun in my pocket. The person was obscured behind random boxes, but his curses indicated he'd found the body.

Either the crew thought I was dead as well, or they didn't care about me at that point. Contemplating the situation, I figured it was probably the latter, since they had bigger problems.

I waited for a while, expecting the ramp to be lowered, but that never happened. "What are they doing up front?" I muttered.

The flight deck had been ominously quiet for a long while. Cautiously, I crawled around and over some of the boxes to make my way to the cockpit door. That was the only other way out. I put my ear to it and stayed quiet. I still couldn't hear anything, but I didn't know how much I would hear through the metal, anyway. Taking the silence as a good sign, I hoped they were all gone. I opened the door slightly and peered in. The cockpit was empty, but the outer hatch had been left open.

As I slowly edged into the flight deck, I heard men talking at the foot of the ladder that led from the hatch down to the ground. I couldn't make out much, but it sounded like they were expecting reinforcements pretty soon.

Their voices faded as they all walked into the increasing shadows surrounding the derelict runway. At that point, I felt I could make my escape. Climbing down the ladder quietly, I gently set my feet on the desert gravel. Keeping to the shadows, I ran to the brush along the runway to get out of sight of any thugs.

Another group of guys came up toward me. I tried to hide. The few cactuses in the area made me pause, but hiding behind a cactus or a bush wouldn't give much protection. I had to laugh at myself for even considering it.

Right then, my phone rang. "I am having the worst luck!" I muttered to myself. In all that I'd been through, I hadn't thought of silencing the phone. I didn't even bother to look at the caller I.D.

I hunkered down for a moment and switched the phone to vibrate, stuffing it back in my pocket. From where I crouched, an outcropping of rocks wasn't too far away. The approaching bad guys were now alerted to me, so I headed as fast as I could toward it.

The thought struck me that these were the reinforcements the thugs back at the foot of the ladder had mentioned. The suave, foreign-sounding man's voice carried across the distance as he told them, "Go bring her back. You should be able to handle one woman." He sounded more inconvenienced than angry.

The gun was still in my pocket, though I wished for John's expertise. The bad guys began to close in on my hiding spot. If there is a next time, I vowed that I would definitely take a federal gun training course. I could have kicked myself for not paying attention, but I had seen John replace a clip in the past. I took the gun from my pocket and hurried to position the outcropping of rocks in between me and the thugs.

As they advanced, I aimed at whoever was closest. They'd fall back and take cover. Then they'd move forward again. With shards of rock exploding around me, it was all I could do to keep them at a distance. Even though I lacked skill, I at least bought myself a little time. Then a thought made me shiver. How many bullets does this gun have? I hadn't thought about it at the time. I had been too grossed out to feel around the crushed body for extra ammunition. Ewww.

Chapter 8

The bad guys were advancing again. All I wanted to do was keep them at a distance, but when I fired one time, I heard a curse. They all started heading toward the man, so I presumed he'd been wounded. While it bothered me that I'd hurt somebody, I needed to buy a little time because, by that point, my gun was almost empty.

When the ammunition was gone, I didn't know what else to do. The gun was useless, so I just left it there among the rocks. Things were getting bleak. Hopefully, no other bad guys would show up.

The setting sun added to my feeling of desperation. It was getting dark and I was out of options. Listening intently, I began to hear gunfire. The bad guys started paying more attention to what was going on around the plane, behind them. It was a relief when they eventually began moving away.

That was when the helicopters arrived. They were really quiet, too, like the ones that had helped John with Arty's cell.

People with dark uniforms were busy rounding up some of the thugs. "The good guys are here!" I cheered. It looked like total chaos, but I was happy to see it.

The last time John and I had met up with other NSA people, he told me to keep my hands in view. I carefully came out from behind the rocks and put my arms out to the side to show I was unarmed.

Sometimes being invisible is not such a bad thing. When some of the good guys did notice me, they all raised their weapons at my approach. I slowed down and kept my hands outstretched. Finally, I saw the one person I had wanted to see.

John stepped over and waved the others off. He had taken off his jacket, and I could see a dark stain of blood across his white suit shirt. It didn't look fresh, but he'd been wounded. That was probably why he hadn't answered my earlier calls.

My attention narrowed to John and the fact that his arm was bandaged. I hadn't even noticed that my hand had gone over my mouth at the thought that he potentially could have died. The idea literally sucked the air out of my lungs. I couldn't breathe. I ran toward him.

"I suppose I shouldn't be mad at you after all!" I said when I got close enough to talk to him.

With all my focus on John, I didn't notice the activity that was still happening nearby. One of my abductors came up from behind and grabbed me. He placed a cold muzzle firmly against my head. He yelled to the law enforcement people, "Back away or she dies!" That familiar accent made me shiver.

All I could think of to say was, "It's you again!" Rather anticlimactic, but it's hard to come up with a snappy line in the heat of the moment.

Everything after that seemed to go in slow motion. All the others began to turn and raise their guns.

I fixated on the look of concern in John's eyes, and heard him call to the others, "He's got a hostage! Hold your fire!"

The guy threw his arm across my throat. My toes barely grazed the gravel as he roughly yanked me in front of him. He dragged me backward.

My breathing became difficult. I started to gasp, feeling faint. My eyesight was getting darker. Was that just twilight?

What could I do? I decided I'd just relax and make this bad guy carry me. He had to shift to support my weight. That allowed me to get some air. I slumped even further, and my feet finally scraped across the desert sand. The man mumbled, "Why aren't you…?" When I stumbled forward, he couldn't stop my motion and fell with me.

After that, things happened in a blur. While my captor was distracted, John stepped forward to see what he could do. When I sank, he aimed a kick to knock the weapon from the attacker's hand. I was light-headed and still trying to get some air, but I stayed down on the ground. I was certainly very glad John was good at action.

The suave broker gave up at that point. I couldn't figure that one out. Other team members surrounded the man and took him away.

John secured the broker's weapon then quickly turned his attention to me. He put out a hand and helped me to my feet. I have to admit, I didn't need to cling to him quite as long as I did, but why not take advantage of the situation? I deserved it!

He just looked at me and sighed unhappily. He said in a controlled tone of voice, "Didn't you put a phone in with the UAV parts? That's what you texted me. Why would you get into the plane with the phone already there giving information?"

Before I could get anything out, he continued, "Part of spycraft is learning when to let the technology work for you."

I explained, "I didn't deliberately sneak on the plane. They captured me and forced me onboard. That's why I was there."

He was only slightly mollified, but he continued, "I recall telling you to get out of there and let us handle it."

"Well, you weren't there at the shop or the little airfield. It wasn't my fault I'd been dragged into it. At that point I felt I had to do something. Putting the phone in with the parts was helpful, you have to admit it. After I'd been caught and tied with a flexi cuff, I couldn't exactly get out of the plane," I said in my defense. "Do you remember your last phone call just before we took off? You said you were on your way, but I didn't know when. You said I shouldn't anger them. When I got free, I retrieved the gun from the squished bad guy. After the plane landed, there was no one around. I got out of there and, well, here I am."

He looked aghast as I recounted the death of the unfortunate man on the plane. Even though he shook his head, he had that little lopsided smile on his face. "What am I going to do with you?"

Oh, I love it when his eyes crinkle! Yet, even though he was frustrated, his smile told me he wasn't mad at me. He was more concerned for my welfare.

"What would you do without me?" I teasingly retorted. "Besides, didn't I ever tell you it's not a good idea to worry me? When I couldn't get any response to my calls and texts, you really alarmed me. I thought that was gunfire in the background the last time we spoke. What if you'd gotten killed?" I don't know how I became so bold, but I reached up to run my thumb over a smudge of dirt on his cheek.

He reached over to tuck a stray strand of hair behind my ear. "You had me worried, too." After a thoughtful moment, the look on his face softened. He leaned his forehead against mine and said, "You're going to be the death of me, or of yourself. You're not bulletproof!"

If this had been a romance story, that might have been a good ending, but my life is hardly a novel.

The other team members were busy rounding up the bad guys and inspecting the boxes in the cargo plane. Someone called out to John.

"Of course, you have to get back to work," I told him reluctantly. "No storybook kiss," I grumbled under my breath. "We were so close, too."

John might have heard that. I thought I saw a little smile play on his lips before he turned to the others and got engrossed in work.

By then, it was completely dark. Someone took me over to a hastily made fire. With a spare jacket over my shoulders, I began to relax a little.

***

The helicopters landed, the bad guys were escorted aboard, and finally, John came back to check on me. "I have to go with the rest of my team," he said.

If I wanted answers, there wouldn't be another chance. I took a deep breath and fired off what was uppermost on my mind. "What was with that UCAV from the rest stop, and who were those guys who stole it? And how is that data thief involved?"

His eyes crinkled as he considered the questions. "As for the aircraft, you never saw that and you aren't going to speak or write about it. Ever." That was more a statement than a question.

I cocked an eyebrow inquiringly at him, but he continued. "And the men were..." Here, he hesitated. He looked hard at me, and said quietly, "Let's just say they were probably connected with Ravens Eye Group and wanted to use the prototype's capabilities. It doesn't take much imagination to see they could use it for running drugs and advancing their agenda."

"That's disturbing," I agreed. "But how did these bad guys know about this aircraft? Wasn't it supposed to be secret?"

John gave a worried look. "That's something NSA is working on right now. We expect to get some answers eventually, but it'll take some time to sort everything out."

"Could it have been an inside job?" I said, not considering the consequences of that question. "The foreign guy seemed to be giving the orders. I have a feeling that he is somewhere at the head of things. What about those two agents?"

John looked uneasy. "Let us handle that. Getting any deeper into this wouldn't be safe for you to do, believe me," he said. Then, his expression softened. "For now, let's get you back where you're supposed to be." He stepped closer to me and extended the arm that hadn't been wounded.

I took it and smiled. As he helped me up I had to ask him, "You never told me what you were doing the last time we talked. Did I really hear gunshots?"

"Well," he said, and seemed to collect his thoughts. "There was a firefight. Your supposition that it was an inside job was correct. Someone was leaking information to the Ravens Eye guys. We got one person that we know was working with them, at least. That's how I got shot."

He shook his head and moved on to another topic. "It was helpful to have their movements tracked, but you could have been hurt," he said sternly, looking at me with concern in his eyes. He turned to me and said, "Thanks to your help, we've gotten this group. Next time, however, let us handle it!"

I smiled. "Thank you. I'm happy to know that you're including me as well when you say, 'We got them.' Next time, you can definitely handle it. If there is a next time, that is."

He reflected on my statement for a minute and nodded in agreement. He took my elbow and we walked together in silence.

The solid feel of his arm in mine was enjoyable and I took a few moments to savor it. Then he led me toward one of the waiting helicopters.

He told me, "I'll see you later. For now, *try* to stay out of trouble." He walked over to the other waiting helicopter. Then he stopped and looked back at me. His parting glance told me exactly what I wanted to know. He was thinking about me, too.

This time, it wasn't going to end the way it had before, with each of us going our separate ways. Chalk it up to the adrenaline that was still in my system, but I found the guts to quickly walk over to him. I placed my hands on his chest and leaned in close to him.

It may have been an unwise and impulsive move, but I had fantasized about giving him a deep and meaningful kiss for a while. Yet, as satisfying as I dreamed it might be, I chickened out and gave him a quick peck on the cheek instead. The slight stubble on his face rubbed my lips. I felt his heartbeat speed up.

The look on his face was priceless. He was totally taken by surprise.

I loved it! I told him, "You'd better take care of yourself, or I'll worry. You've learned you don't want me worried." I smiled and said, "Till we meet again!" This time my boldness had paid off!

***

The helicopter took me to the airfield in Idaho, where I got my car back. It was a better idea to return to the original plan of the Seattle relocation. In Idaho, they decided to put me in a secure room overnight. Of course, it was to be sure I was safe after what had happened to me. However, I have a feeling it was also to make sure I didn't go on any more unauthorized adventures before I made it to the classified site. They needn't have worried!

Even though I was exhausted, sleeping was difficult that night. I kept mulling over all the things I'd been through and all the things I needed to do.

The next morning, I savored a rejuvenating jolt from a double-shot espresso before continuing my travels. After those nights sleeping in the car, I still wasn't fully recharged, but the cup of coffee would certainly help.

The little outdoor bistro table in the warm morning sunshine was enjoyable. Thumbing through a news app on my phone, a very interesting article caught my eye.

Just as I started reading, someone sat down across from me at my table. It was John! He had showered and changed, but he still looked tired. His arm was in a sling, but his smile showed me he was OK.

My heart sped up and I couldn't help the big smile I gave him. We both took a sip of coffee and sat in companionable silence for a minute before talking. Many questions were on my mind.

"Have you found out anything about the information broker with the accent and what he was doing?"

John's lips curved up in a smile. "After coffee, we'll take a walk."

When we were done, he took my arm. Together, we strode down the sidewalk. He led me away from the morning crowd. It was a pleasurable sensation to be close enough beside him that I could feel the rumble of his voice.

"NSA has begun to unravel the names of the members of this section of Ravens Eye Group. We'll find out who was responsible for the theft of the prototype craft soon."

"So, is the suave data thief a bad guy, or is he working for your organization? I couldn't figure out which," I prodded. "He seemed to expect that I would do something... counter his move, or react a specific way, and I didn't."

Of course, John wouldn't say any more about it than, "He's been informative." I figured I wouldn't press him any more on that subject.

"Is there any news about how these thieves got the inside information on the UCAV?"

John held up his good hand and said, "Investigations take time." I gave him an annoyed look. He relented and said, "Their information was so accurate, it must have been leaked. That's why they knew what we were doing, which is unfortunate."

His look of pain and betrayal resonated with me. John had been misled by a co-worker he had trusted with his life. I had been fooled by Arty's duplicity. Treachery like that can shake a person to the core.

"You called Bob Smart to assist you at the motel, I recall." A chilling thought occurred to me. "If he had taken over for you back then, when I first learned of Ravens Eye Group, what would have happened?"

John hadn't ever spoken of it. He ran his fingers through his hair in frustration and said, "We're still piecing things together. He might not have done anything, but it was a good thing you didn't hang around the rest area much longer. That other guy might have killed you." I could tell that my second encounter with Smart bothered him.

I didn't want to dwell any further on unpleasant subjects, but there was one last item I had to discuss. I passed my phone to him, where the news item covering the recent events was displayed, so he could read it.

He glanced at it and handed my phone back to me, but didn't immediately say anything. The article hadn't surprised him.

I read from the item, "'Witnesses in the area relate hearing numerous mysterious booms and seeing unexplained flashes in the sky. The local military base reports that the noises and lights are just common occurrences, resulting from a routine training exercise using flares.' That's what they're calling it? Really?" I was surprised. "Having lived through the actual event, that article's version of the incident is hilarious," I chuckled.

I noticed John was trying to keep a straight face. I had to ask, "Was that the best cover-up story they could provide?"

He just smiled that little half-smile and said, "It's just standard procedure. Simple explanations are easier to dismiss if they're ever disproved." As he said that, he reached over and slipped something else in my hand. It was my old phone, the one I had used for tracking the drone parts.

He looked pensive and said, "I have to get to work," but he didn't move. He looked in my eyes. "At times, it's easy to lose track of why I do this, especially with recent events concerning that agent. Yet it seems that every time you're there, you restore my focus, or at least keep me on my toes! You've been good for me, when you haven't driven me nuts."

The look in his eyes told me what he meant. All I could do was turn into his embrace and hold him as tightly as I could. As I did so, I couldn't help but notice how good it felt and how well we fit together. I didn't know what to say, so I put into that embrace what words couldn't convey.

Slowly, he bent his head and put his lips against mine. This time I put my arms around him and took full advantage of his closeness. I breathed in his aftershave, and savored the rise and fall of his solid chest. It was satisfying to have him eagerly kiss me, and I kissed him back just as passionately. I didn't want it to end.

Our hearts eventually stopped racing. We held on to each other for a while. The problems of the world faded long enough for us to enjoy a moment of peace together. As he pulled back, I moved my hands to his firm chest and took a breath.

"Wow," he said, and we both had big smiles. He put his forehead against mine and told me, "I really do have to go, for now."

All I could say was, "I understand."

That was the point when I knew, deep down inside, that we had to be together, no matter what. Making things work would be hard, but I was willing to try, for him.

Just as I care about the quality of the job I do, his job is important to him. He has a lot riding on his shoulders, and he cares about the people working with him. His actions have monumental consequences. I wanted to help him create a better world, not just for everyone, but for a shared future we both could enjoy. Just as I wanted and needed to be there for him, I needed him there for me.

I looked forward to the next time we'd meet. At least, I sincerely hoped we would see each other again. Hopefully, next time it wouldn't involve guns, and bullets, and dangerous situations!

Chapter 9

After the turmoil of the last adventure had faded, I tried to fashion a new life for myself, but my thoughts returned to John. I always longed for more time with him. However, I forgot that the old saying is true. "Be careful what you wish for, you might just get it." Unfortunately, it never turns out the way you think.

The new job I'd been transferred into was technical enough to keep me on my toes, but it wasn't as exciting as being with John. It was a paycheck and it kept me concealed in mundane obscurity. "This is for your safety," I was told again and again.

The paycheck could only go so far. The best thing I could say about the inexpensive efficiency unit I found, which was much smaller than my previous apartment, was that it didn't take too long to clean. That was a plus.

Even learning my new job and surroundings didn't keep me from worrying about John. I kept trying to piece together the events I'd been though: the Quantum GPS and the bigger UCAV with the potential for weapons. I couldn't help but shudder at how a group with ruthless intent might put those capabilities together.

Standing in line to get my coffee, or checking out at the grocery store, I'd catch myself looking over my shoulder every now and then. I hoped that John would walk up to me with that little half-grin of his. He was my anchor in this sea of change, as well as my protector. In spite of having been sucked into the craziness that was John's work, I couldn't help wanting to see him more.

The rare occasions when John and I could get together were enjoyable, but the feeling of wariness that had been with me since being grabbed by the foreign guy persisted. I didn't know if he was really a bad guy or not, but I dreaded meeting up with him again.

John and I had discussions about the aspects of my situation that were hard for me to accept. He stressed that there were adaptations I needed to accept for safety reasons. He suggested I should keep myself occupied and find activities that would keep my brain engaged, like taking some classes.

***

Days came and went. When he had time, John came by to visit. That was really the best part of this whole relocation. At first, we just had coffee and talked things through. He was a good listener, and I was fascinated to hear about his life.

We both had to adapt. I had to get used to his intense focus. John had to get used to my sense of humor. After a while, we'd progressed to having dinner and seeing what was on the TV in this modest-sized town. On his visits, he'd take me to do some of his training exercises and favorite outdoor activities. We saw each other as often as we could. Holding hands soon became cuddling on the couch.

One evening, we were enjoying some time together. Just as he was leaning me back on the couch to deepen his intoxicating kiss, we were interrupted by his phone. All I could hear was his side of the conversation. "Yes. No, that won't work. We'll see you tonight then. Just give us an hour. Yes, I will be bringing someone. Now, don't go there." He told them goodbye and thumbed the connection closed.

"Don't tell me, let me guess," I grumbled. "You have to go on another secret mission."

"No. Well, soon, but not yet. Tonight, I have a mission for you," he said, stroking my cheek.

I waited for him to elaborate, and when he didn't, I poked him playfully in his ribs. "Out with it. Who do I have to kill?" I meant it as a joke, but he looked aghast. He still has to adapt to my wisecracks.

"Well, it seems my parents are in town and want to get together. They said they could meet me at the swanky restaurant in their hotel. Would you like to come along? With their schedule, tonight is about the only time we all can meet. You don't mind, do you? Otherwise, I can cancel it, but…"

"I'm just worried about their expectations. At this stage, it might be a bit early to be meeting the parents. At least, I can tell you my parents would be making plans for our future children in this situation. I don't want to put any pressure on you, but if we go together, I'm sure there will be many questions. There are things we still need to discuss before we face the inquiry from our parents. I just don't want to rush things before we're ready."

He stroked my face. "Well, I'm an action kind of guy. I believe in doing what I think is right instead of hiding or beating around the bush. You've become important to me." At that statement, he hesitated. "You're the only one who has ever gotten this close. This is an important relationship boundary. The timing may not be ideal, but we can get through it, wouldn't you agree?"

"You *are* important to me, too. As long as you're OK with it, we can get through it. If I can go through guns, bombs and bullets for you I can do this, too, but believe me, you'll owe me!" I winked. "As for that boundary, we were about to get there…" I spoiled the assertion by blushing when I thought of the *really* personal level we had almost reached!

***

We got ready and went out to meet with his parents, who were already at the restaurant. It was a very fancy place. There's still a part of me that still feels uncomfortable in the spotlight.

On first seeing John's parents, I assumed they would be conservative and stuffy. As awkward as I felt in the restaurant, I felt even more self-conscious when I was introduced to them. I moved in close to give his dad a hug, just as he extended his hand to shake mine. After that, I moved to shake his mother's hand, and she tried to give me an awkward hug. Not the best first impression!

Once we all got to talking, they were actually quite pleasant. His parents, Stanley and Constance, were charming people. While Stanley was in the military, they had traveled extensively. Now they vacationed in different exotic spots around the world. They were genuinely interested in what was going on in our lives and how we met.

At one point, John needed to take a phone call and stepped away from the table.

They saw that I was concerned, and Constance confided in me. "John probably wouldn't talk about it, but he has a personal reason for getting into his line of work. His job is important to him." Stanley gave his wife a quelling glance, but she made a conciliatory gesture to him. "I know better than to give out specific information. She's probably figured that much out already." She turned to me and continued, "Not that he's told us a lot, either. It's one of those accommodations that must be made."

Constance talked about their younger days. "How worried I got when my Stanley had orders to go off to some unknown place! Sometimes it was hard but, oh, he cut quite the figure back then! Of course, he still does, in my estimation."

The loving looks they gave each other melted my heart.

"We can see you're important to John. Be strong for him. He can't tell you all of what he does, but I remember how it was for my Stanley. Let him talk when he wants to and be understanding when he can't. Stay beside him. You'll help John immensely just by being that support."

"I was a lucky man to have that support from you, my dear." Stanley smiled at her and gently kissed her knuckles.

They looked at each other and held hands. It was one of those moments that made me hope that John and I might be lucky enough to have that, too.

***

After dinner, John and I went back to my place and picked up where we'd left off. We started feeding each other little treats, like chocolate covered cherries. I astounded myself when he held one to my mouth and I gently bit the top of the candy off.

As I used my tongue to carefully scoop the cherry from its chocolate shell to my lips, I noticed that he was watching me avidly. John's eyebrows rose in interest. His eyes locked with mine and he edged closer to me. We went from chocolate covered cherries to chocolate kisses. Soon, we went from kisses to fireworks! That man knows how to use his weapon, if you know what I mean.

Afterward, John gave me some unwanted news. "I need to go deal with something." He didn't tell, and I knew better than to ask, but it probably had something to do with Ravens Eye. What rotten timing. This mysterious but important mission was yet another reason to dislike those bad guys! As Constance had told me, "You may never know about certain parts of his life, but be there for him."

What a disappointment, just when things were getting good! He finished packing a spare outfit into an overnight bag and tucked his shaving kit in. He came over and gave me a deep kiss. I was missing his little half-smile as soon as he walked out the door.

While he was away, I became extremely aware of my surroundings. At work one afternoon, I heard someone talking with my boss as they walked down the hall. Was that the data thief I'd met before? What was he doing here? Wasn't he supposed to be in prison?

My apprehension rose as I peeked around the corner. By that time, they'd moved on. I could barely see them, but the height and build were similar. I could have sworn I'd heard the cultured inflections of the mysterious guy. "Just overactive imagination," I chided myself, and I went back to my work.

It was a relief when my workday finally ended. Leaving quickly that afternoon, I warily looked over my shoulder to see if the information broker was anywhere around. No one even remotely resembled him. Once I got away from the building I pulled my phone out of my purse and called John.

Naturally, he didn't answer. He still hadn't returned from his latest mission, although he had expected to be back before this. I didn't want to interrupt his job with an unfounded suspicion, so I hung up and headed home.

Once there, I threw my keys on the little kitchenette table in my tiny apartment. Just as I reached for my cell phone to recharge it, the vibration of an incoming text message startled me. It wasn't from John, because he would have called, not texted me. The message was, "We have John. You and I must talk. Get out of your apartment *now*."

At this point, I was starting to panic. What kind of trouble was John in? What could I do to help him? Frantically grabbing my purse and keys, I locked the door and ran down the hallway. I went outside and thought better of getting in my car. Walking as calmly as I could, I went to a nearby coffee shop. Inside, I stood in line and scanned the area.

A man sauntered up behind me. He quietly said, "Feel free to get some coffee. We must sit down and talk."

A chill went down my spine as I instantly recognized that voice. Quickly turning around, I made eye contact with him. The man was elegantly dressed and, with his bronzed coloration, he was quite good looking. It was too bad he was the dreaded information broker.

"Well, well, it's you again," I said. Unfortunately my voice was a little too shaky to pull off that bravado convincingly. "I suppose I could get some coffee, but what if I just leave?"

"That would not be recommended. Not if you want John to stay alive."

With that threat, I complied. Of course, the first thing I said once we were seated was, "Where is he? He'd better be OK."

The suave guy just said, "John is only a little worse for wear, but alive."

"What do you mean? What have you done with my man?" I was getting frantic. My head whipped around to look for John, but he wasn't there.

His eyebrow rose slightly, but he said, "He is safe for now."

"How did you find where I live? And how did you know I came here?" I asked, my voice rising.

He stated firmly, "Calm yourself, and do stop glancing around. He is not here. I knew where you were and that you came here to this coffee shop because I have had you watched."

My eyes narrowed at that.

He looked me in the eye and told me, "Even as we speak, there are people going through your apartment."

"What could I possibly have that anybody would want?" I said defensively.

He tipped his head to concede the point and told me, "Of that, I am not sure."

Despite getting more frightened by the minute, I looked at him and huffed, "I don't trust you. Weren't you arrested? For all I know, you're some pirate or something. How do you know there are people in my apartment in the first place?"

"I know because I sent them." His bold statement forced me to pay attention. "I simply needed to give them something to do so we could talk without their interference. To be clear, no, I am no pirate. I just work for them."

His voice dropped, forcing me to listen quietly to hear him. "This is more serious than you imagine, but I am trying to help both you and John."

That left me momentarily speechless.

"Dear lady, allow me to introduce myself. I am Alejandro Vargas. John and I have known each other for some time. NSA and my organization have a long-standing cooperative agreement. My job is to gain access to information about Ravens Eye Group and what they are doing. What I learn gets shared with NSA. The news of my arrest was simply to confirm my cover story. If you would prefer to get John back alive, you need to cooperate," Vargas said emphatically.

Before I could even assimilate that, he told me, "Your association with John recently came to the attention of Ravens Eye. That has led me to you, which is another reason for the unfortunate violation of your apartment. I needed to maintain the appearance of checking you out as Ravens Eye wishes."

I thought back to when I helped John identify pictures and find the Quantum GPS unit. "What if I tell NSA about this?" I asked with as much boldness as I could muster. "Surely, they'd help him."

Vargas said, "Even if you did contact someone, it is doubtful whether they would consider any information you gave them to be reliable, since you have no proof. It is also quite possible that there are informants within NSA. Telling them could alert Ravens Eye and compromise things further."

As incredible as it sounded, what he'd told me seemed truthful, especially when I thought of Bob Smart. However, I needed to be convinced. "It's hard to believe you. After all, you did try to kill me back in the desert!"

He smiled at that. "Subterfuge. Circles within circles to hide the goal, my dear. As for trying to kill you before, if I were less proficient than I am, you certainly would be dead," he preened. "John knows my expertise. You see, he and I have been through a lot together. We both owe each other our lives, many times over, and I want to help him as much as I can. That is why I will help you in rescuing him. It is the only way he will survive."

The suave man elaborated, "Ravens Eye Group has people inside various organizations. They even watch their own people. With such levels of secrecy, many will not have received enough information to see you as a threat, so you would be perfect." He explained, "I know that you have worked together with John. The information is surprisingly sparse. I can only presume you are his associate, or perhaps you are in some deep cover assignment. I must commend you on a very thorough cover story."

"Wait a minute. I'm supposed to rescue John? I'm no spy. I just help him. Well, as much as possible. I can imagine he'd put that differently."

Vargas looked unexpectedly surprised at my admission that I just assist John, but he nodded. "John was supposed to make contact with someone who insisted he would only meet with John. Things went wrong. At this point it is unclear whether John was set up, but he was captured and the informant was killed."

"Are you sure he's not already dead? This is new to me. What if I'm captured? Will I get help when I need it? It sounds suicidal. Are you sure this will work?" I probed, unconvinced of the soundness of his plan.

He leaned forward. "It very well might get you killed if you are unwise. To maintain my cover, I must not interfere to help him or show that I have information concerning him. Your help will be essential in this because he knows and trusts you, and you can do what I cannot."

"OK, I have to accept the fact that you're a double agent, but I don't even know where to go," I said, attempting to wrap my brain around this story of his.

"That is a crude term, but a close enough description of my assignment. You need to go to Sedona. There, with my help, we can free John."

My heart was hammering in my chest and I was probably hyperventilating. This was getting worse by the minute. "How am I supposed to do this?" I stammered. "I assume that by sending me to Sedona, you're telling me that's where he is."

Vargas just said, "Calm down and finish your coffee. You will be contacted once you arrive at your destination. I will give you all the help I possibly can. Just remember that there will be only so much I can do and my participation must remain concealed. You must be careful who you tell of this trip."

He took my hand and kissed it in an old-world gentlemanly fashion. As he released my hand, he gave me a packet. "The documents in there are good for one week only. Afterward, the information gets deleted. Once these documents vanish, there will be no paper trail. Only certain trusted people in the NSA know about these papers. When they ask for them, give them the documents back when this is done. You can trust me," he said. "However, you should be wary of that boss of yours." He then left quickly.

All right, I could play along. I finished my coffee with trembling hands, and then left the shop. I tried to be as nonchalant as Vargas had been, but probably failed miserably. "Now what should I do? Is it OK to go home yet?" I fretted. I hate not knowing the answers.

Vargas' goons might not be done yet, so I decided to waste a little more time. I found a place in the late afternoon sun to calm my nerves.

If John were here, what would he tell me to do? I sat in the park and pondered my resources. Eventually, I decided it was time to go back home and pack. By that time, the goons were gone and they left very little mess to clean up.

"Vargas is polite, I'll give him that," I said mirthlessly. It was a creepy feeling to know that strangers had been there, going through my clothes. If I hadn't been pressed to get packed, I might have washed all my panties just for my own peace of mind.

I remembered something John had mentioned earlier about keeping explanations simple. It applied in this situation. I decided to text my boss the excuse that I was unexpectedly not feeling well and needed some time off. It would do for a few days.

This would be my first trip to the Southwest. Too bad it wasn't under better circumstances. Packing light, I prepared to catch a cab. I hoped my cover story for work would suffice. If Vargas really worked with John and his people, then would NSA be aware of what I was doing?

I opened the packet. Inside was a plane ticket for a flight this evening and a prepaid credit card. The convincing I.D. startled me. Where Vargas had come up with my picture was a mystery I didn't even want to contemplate. The name read Velma Antwerp.

"Really? At least after a week Velma's documents will be gone."

How much credit was on Velma's card? Not knowing what other expenses to expect, I wanted to refrain from running up a big credit card bill. According to the itinerary, Velma was to fly to Flagstaff, Arizona. How was I to get to Sedona?

The realization hit me that I would owe Vargas, big time, for his help. I could only wonder what the cost of his assistance would be. If it would help John, I'd accept the debt.

***

The trip was a typical coach experience, but I didn't care. After a worry-filled flight, I got off the plane in Flagstaff. Looking around at the unfamiliar airport, I fretted that Vargas hadn't told me if anyone was going to meet me.

Retrieving my small amount of luggage, I walked out to the curb. An older man was standing at the passenger pickup area, holding a sign with my fake name on it. I began to wonder just how deep the spy's connections went.

With misgivings, I walked over to the old man holding the sign and told him, "I'm Velma Antwerp." After seeing my fake identification, he gave a small nod of his head. He took my luggage case and led me to a car. Opening the back door, he seated me like I was a person of importance. That thought made me wonder if I should have been filled in on Velma's background.

When the wizened driver had put my luggage in the trunk, he got behind the wheel and headed into the city. While he navigated the sun-washed streets, I sat back and enjoyed the air conditioning. The views of the city were captivating, but my gratification at seeing someplace new was temporary. I kept thinking of John's situation, and how he was "none the worse for wear," as Vargas had put it. Just how bad was John being treated? I chafed at not knowing the answer.

The old gentleman pulled up to a shuttle station and opened the door. He set my luggage beside me, then he handed me a phone. "It was thought the lady might like to read on her journey." I barely got to thank the old man before he was gone.

The obvious thing to do was to scroll through the apps. The only book listed was Dickens' *Great Expectations*. It was either a very appropriate title for someone with my limited capabilities, or Vargas had a strange sense of humor. I hoped his expectations of me at that point weren't too excessive.

In looking through the e-book, a highlighted note on page seven read: "Go buy a shuttle ticket to Sedona." Despite my confusion, I stood in line and finally made my way up to the booth to purchase the ticket. The person in the ticket booth was the same old man who had driven me to the shuttle station. He ran Velma's credit card and handed me a ticket. Motioning me to where the gate was, he dismissed me and went on to help the next customer.

Scrolling a few pages further through the book, I found additional instructions. "Go into the assigned waiting area and leave the shuttle ticket on the last bench on the right. Then walk away and do not look back." It was a cryptic command, but I could play this game.

I turned around to walk back toward the ticketing area. Even though I wasn't supposed to, I peeked back at the bench to see that a woman had picked up the ticket and was heading over to board the shuttle. She was about my size and height and was dressed much as I was.

That sly devil had planned for it to look like I'd gotten on the shuttle when I really hadn't! I wondered if there was something else to this ploy. Scrolling further through the book, I read, "There will be a car waiting at the Acme car rental agency. Drive to Sedona."

Fortunately, Velma Antwerp had a credit card. I couldn't help myself; I thumbed through the book a little more. Sure enough, there was one last obscure piece of advice from Vargas. "Drive carefully. Follow the map. On it, you will see a marker. Stop off at a place called Jose's Diner. Order the steak or chicken, not the seafood. You will be met when you turn in the car."

Chapter 10

"This situation is straight out of a spy novel. I'm so tired of the convoluted games," I groused to myself once they delivered the rental car. Vargas' reference to circles within circles began to make sense.

After about an hour on the road and a chicken taco at Jose's Diner, I made it to Sedona. The stop at the diner is still a mystery I'm probably happier not trying to solve, though it was nice to have a bit of a rest.

The car was returned, and Vargas himself was there to meet me in front of the rental place. He bent at the waist and kissed my hand.

"You know, a girl could get spoiled with all this gallant treatment," I told him. He just gave a suave smile, like he got that reaction from women all the time.

He took my suitcase and led me to a luxurious sedan. As we got in, he warned me not to trust anyone. "You never know who has been bribed or coerced. Loyalty changes on a daily basis. Every organization has its bureaucracy and red tape. I have done what I can to complicate and obscure what we are doing in order to protect John as much as possible. However, I cannot say how long this ruse will last. His life is in the balance."

"John isn't dead, is he?" I needed some reassurance.

"The situation is stable enough for the moment, but you are the random element they failed to factor into their plans. You are the only one who could tip the balance in his favor. Anyone else's allegiance is always in question."

My heart raced as I thought about Bob Smart and how his leaked information had caused trouble. He had almost gotten John killed. I could only trust that this suave man was telling the truth.

"When things started, John was protecting me. Now, the roles are reversed and I'm somehow supposed to rescue him."

Vargas nodded at my summary of the situation.

The thought of failing John petrified me. The reality that he could be killed was daunting. It was the moment where things became crystal clear. I knew that I had to do this.

"With your assistance, I'll get him out of there," I said with mounting determination. "I'm grateful for the knowledge that John is still alive and for your help. How will we do it?"

Vargas exhaled. "For now, I will take you to my villa. The quickest way to get you close enough is to make it look like I am bringing you into the organization. You will be in disguise, but you must be convincing. Otherwise, we are all dead."

"I'll do my best to play along," I replied. To keep myself from freaking out, I asked, "Tell me again about John's capture."

Vargas explained, "The person requested John come alone. The man had been reliable before. Since he is dead, we can only surmise. Both of them may have been setup. Alternatively, the mole may have deliberately given up John. When Ravens Eye got what they wanted, they no longer needed the mole."

My mind was working on a number of things. What was Ravens Eye's goal? What was I supposed to do to assist? How would a new recruit act? I'm known for asking questions, not my acting ability.

The rest of the ride was filled with a long, uncomfortable silence.

***

At his villa, Vargas parked in a shaded carport and we headed toward the grand entrance.

His home was elegant. I was impressed with its beauty and spaciousness. "I've never seen anything like it. The entryway tilework is reminiscent of Spanish-style architecture, and the stone privacy wall blends in with the desert."

"I am glad you noticed that. It was designed like a villa from my grandparents' country, Spain. He leaned in toward me, and I panicked.

"What am I supposed to do, kiss you?" I whispered to him.

Vargas merely reached out and took the luggage from my hand. He smiled seductively and told me, "Relax! You do not appear to be enjoying yourself. For this to work, you must be convincing." He smiled encouragingly and offered his other arm.

He led me inside and up a sweeping staircase. "A suite has been prepared for you." He opened the door, and placed my bag inside the room. He inclined his head and said, "I must attend to business. For now, please feel free to rest and freshen up."

As he left, I stepped into the lovely suite. It was large, certainly bigger than my apartment. Looking around a little, I indulged my curiosity. Unembarrassed by my nosiness, I opened all of the closet doors. Some of them were empty, but some were full of beautiful day dresses and evening gowns, while others held men's clothing! What was I to make of that? "Does this guy have a lot of guests, or am I in his room?" I could only speculate.

After a quick shower, I was lounging across the bed in a robe I'd found in the closet. I was engrossed in reading *Great Expectations*. The story spoke to me on a deeper level.

The shadows had started lengthening in the room. A knock on the door made me sit upright. I was tense and apprehensive. "Come in," I said timidly.

A gray-haired woman discreetly stuck her head in the door. "I am the housekeeper. Dinner is formal here at the villa. The gowns should be your size. Please feel free to choose one. Señor Vargas requests that you dress and join him downstairs. Dinner will be served in an hour."

"Just how did Mr. Vargas find my size?" I asked, but the woman didn't answer, quietly closing the door after her. Then my mind started working on the information that I would have to dress for dinner!

I looked at the gowns, and picked what I hoped would be nice, but not at all seductive. It was bright and flattering and totally beyond my usual "beige and boring – hide in plain sight" style.

The housekeeper returned a little later and helped me with my hair. When I was ready, I looked at myself in the mirror. The image of me in the lovely gown and sleek hair-do looked unlike the "plain, invisible" woman I was. The difference was unbelievable.

Would this irrevocably change me from the "ordinary" person I was, once this was over? What if I couldn't go back to the way I've always been? I bit my lip and worried.

Downstairs in the banquet hall, I briefly hesitated. The grandeur of the room struck me. Despite the beautiful gown I wore, I felt out of place. The room was opulent, with touches of gold and red on the walls and tablecloth. The large dining table was made of dark wood in a heavy, Spanish style. It was certainly way too big for just two people. Vargas was seated at the head of the long table. Fortunately, I was seated at his right hand, or we would never have heard each other.

He was a gracious host, allaying some of my nervousness with fascinating stories about the food we were enjoying. I tried to go light on the wine to maintain a clear head.

After dinner, he poured us both after-dinner drinks and we took them out to the terrace. Just as I was getting comfortable with the situation, he leaned in and said, "Tell me of your life plans."

I deflected the question with a general answer of, "I don't really know. It's been hard enough just trying to get by..."

He continued probing, "What about your plans with John?"

"I'm uncomfortable discussing that. I'm not really sure anyway." I knew that long-term goals with John were only dreams and hopes at this point. How much did this man actually know, and how much should I trust him? I couldn't answer those questions.

He saw my hesitation and continued, quite boldly, "You do realize, my dear, that John can never be totally open and honest with you because there will always be things he just cannot divulge. Are you prepared to accept that from him?"

The nerve! I raised my chin and looked at him steadily. I stated in a cool tone, "I value John's *friendship*, and he has mine, as well. Trust is a good foundation for any relationship. As for any plans, I don't know what the future may hold."

I emphasized the word friendship to indicate that there was a line in this conversation that I wouldn't cross. I didn't foresee how soon that foundation between John and me would be put to the test, however.

Vargas seemed placated by my answer. Perhaps even a little bit saddened, but satisfied. I got the impression that he had put me through an important assessment. He finished his drink and took my hand. As he helped me to my feet, he kissed the back of my hand and called for the housekeeper to lead me to my room.

"Good night," I said to Vargas, grateful to be leaving that strange interrogation.

Once in my room, I quickly got ready for bed and flopped down on the silky sheets. It had been a long and stressful day. That last, puzzling conversation with Vargas left me on edge. Had I been dismissed after having failed his questions, or had I passed? Wondering about it gave me an uneasy feeling.

Later, I must have dozed off, because something awakened me. The clock showed that I had slept only a few hours. Getting back to sleep wouldn't be easy, so I wandered downstairs, looking around the quiet villa. Was John being held here at Vargas' estate? The sooner I could find him and leave the better. I wanted to be done with dangerous spy games.

Some doors led to other rooms. Fortunately, I never ran into Vargas or any of his staff. My cheeks reddened at the thought of what they might think of my nosiness! One door led to the kitchen. After checking that one out, and getting a quick snack, I learned the kitchen door was a dead end.

Another door led down a dim hallway to an empty security control room. I ventured inside. The small conference area had some chairs and a table, but on one wall was a mirror. Putting a finger up to inspect it, I noticed a gap between my finger and the reflection, and knew it was a two-way mirror. On TV, they show them used in interrogation rooms. There was probably another room behind this one, so people could see in. I saw no other door, though.

Walking back through the security control room, the bank of monitors caught my eye. They were all turned off. I turned them on, and various rooms of the estate were displayed. I was relieved to learn that the suite I was using wasn't one being watched.

Other monitors displayed various outdoor areas around the estate. The last screen revealed a stark, shadowy cell made of cinderblock walls.   I watched as a door was opened from a dark hall and a man was shoved into the cell.

That got my attention.   "That can't be John," I said, aghast. I looked closer and my heart stopped at the realization that it was him.   He appeared stiff, but he was moving.   "You're alive and conscious, at least," I said to the image.   I breathed a sigh of relief.

Movement outside the door to the security control room got my attention.   I decided it did no good to try to hide.   Vargas stepped through the door and stopped, startled to see me.   Standing my ground, I pointed to the monitor of the darkened cell room.   I looked accusingly at Vargas and asked, "Have you just come from interrogating John?"

Vargas was puzzled at that question.   He looked me straight in the eye and told me, "No."

"That *is* John on this monitor.   I watched him being put into his cell, right before you walked in."

Vargas looked at first startled, then angry.   He closed the door to the center and sat down with a worried look on his face. Motioning for me to sit in the chair at the adjoining station, he spoke quietly and quickly.   "John is being held elsewhere, in another building far from here.   I have been able to tap into their security system to get a feed.   That is what you have been watching."   He reached over to turn it off.   "Ravens Eye Group must not be alerted to the fact that I am aware of certain developments.   You must not, under any circumstances, mention anything about what you have seen to anyone, even my staff."

I nodded.   "This is a dangerous game you're playing."

Nodding, he went on to say, "Things have gotten more complicated and deadly.   If they are allowing others to interrogate him, even despite my demand that I should handle the questioning, my position within the organization could be more precarious than I previously thought.   We must proceed with extreme caution."

When he looked at me, he probably saw someone with a "deer in the headlights" look.   He took my hands in his and told me, "It will take a lot of fortitude and bravery on your part if you hope to rescue him.   We need to do so quickly."

I was frightened, but I responded, "I hope you have a plan, because I don't know what to do."

He said, "I will be able to get you to where John is being held, but you will have to take it from there. Both our lives are in your hands. I have every confidence that you are up to the task."

I took a deep breath and said, "I can only hope so."

He stood up and motioned for me to follow him. We walked out of the control room together. As he closed and locked the door, he put my arm in his. He spoke quietly, as though he couldn't even trust his own security. "I will do my best to help. As a new recruit, you could look around to familiarize yourself with the building. It would be a reason for you to be in some of the less sensitive sections. However, John is being held further inside the place. You will have to make your way there on your own."

We walked back to the living area of the house, conversing quietly about how I'd have to look different to confuse the bad guys. We were so involved in deciding what I should do to alter my looks that I didn't even realize where we had ended up until he motioned for me to go into my room. I wondered if he might ask to come in, but he didn't try to take advantage of the situation.

"We will talk again in the morning before we leave," Vargas said. To my relief, he left.

What would be expected of me? Could I actually do what was necessary to find John, and free him, and not get us all killed? Those questions weighed on me the rest of the night.

Chapter 11

A sharp knock on my door in the early morning roused me from a troubled sleep. It was the housekeeper, ready to help get me prepared for the day's agenda.

She guided me in the selection of a classy, but subdued, suit. The color was of muted desert tones, but the pattern had brighter Southwest accents to keep it from being like my usual dull office attire. She pulled my hair back, and a dark wig in a sleek bob was placed on my head. I put some brown-tinted contacts in my eyes. My chic makeup and clothes completed the look so well, I almost didn't recognize myself. The image that looked back was a professional and sophisticated woman; almost a contemporary Jackie O.

Vargas noticed the transformation and cast an approving glance at the results. We shared a tense, hurried breakfast. Rescue plans were discussed, discarded, and furiously revised. We covered questions like how I was going to rescue John, without getting him killed or blowing Vargas' cover.

Soon, we were off to the building where John was being held. The beautiful scenery passed in an underappreciated blur. I was fearful that John would be further injured from additional interrogations.

Our destination was a bland building that looked plain enough to discourage much scrutiny. From the outside, it was just an average business or light-industrial building set among the desert hills, with ample parking surrounding the front and sides.

Vargas offered me his arm and we went inside. I still couldn't figure him out. If he was going to help me, he wasn't all bad. He and John had a long-standing association, so I decided to trust him. I sincerely hoped that things wouldn't end badly, because if they did, it would be disastrous for all of us. No pressure!

Vargas gave me an encouraging glance as I clutched his arm a bit tighter than necessary.

We walked across the parking lot. He led me from the main lobby into what looked like a security control room, much like the one in his estate.

I tried not to appear too blatant about looking around while paying attention to his explanations.

He efficiently ensured that I was checked in and issued a temporary visitor identification card. This badge had a different name, to go along with my altered appearance. Now the name was Hepsiba Hapsburg. Yes, it would go along with the more refined, fashionable persona I had adopted, but something less memorable would have been better.

Vargas spoke in commanding terms to some of the people working there in the control room. He guided me out the door and we walked further into the stronghold.

"I need to deal with work. Make sure everyone can see that," he said, indicating my new I.D. He deliberately enunciated, "You can wait in this area till I get back," and gave a little nod of his head and left.

The plan was that I'd go see what I could find from there. Giving Vargas enough time to go down the hall, I left to look around.

Walking down one drab hallway after another, I quietly checked door after door. Being quiet and not calling attention to myself were things I was good at doing. They came in handy here.

A few times, people in lab coats passed me as I walked down the hallway. Since they were deep in conversations, they didn't notice me. I slipped in through a handy door to disappear. One entrance led to a closet, but the other was some sort of lab. It could be interesting. Besides, what's the worst that could happen? If they caught me, I might get taken to where John was held.

To further blend in, I put on a lab coat I found hanging up while looking around the workroom. Then, I noticed something draped across a mannequin standing in the corner. It was some sort of strange vest, green and mottled like military camouflage I've seen. It looked different, but I thought it might be important. It didn't seem to be fashion design. I chuckled at the thought.

Examining it closer, I noticed that there were little buttons along one area of the vest. Of course, I had to check it out to know what they were for. The buttons clicked when I pressed them, much like those on a piece of electronics. So far, they didn't seem to do much, though it was a good thing that they didn't fire missiles!

Voices in the hallway outside the lab signaled that people were approaching. Putting the vest back for now, I chose a random door. It was another closet, but I could hear the conversation pretty well.

The unknown people were talking about how they were only able to obtain the vest. "The Talos suit with stealth capability will be carefully studied. This technology, if adapted, will be useful for other things."

That word must be an acronym for a high-tech device. These bad guys like their acronyms as much as the government does. Adapting something like this device with its capabilities to other applications wasn't a friendly idea. The situation I had gotten myself into was even more dangerous than I had thought.

While waiting for the lab workers to leave, I pondered what the acronym T.A.L.O.S. could mean. Totally Atrocious Lack of Style seemed to fit! It was snarky, but amusing.

The voices eventually receded from the lab, and I was left alone with the strange vest with the electronic buttons that did who knew what. Looking around the thing, I noticed stenciling that indicated this was part of a Tactical Assault Light Operator Suit. I tried it on. It was a little large for me. It was probably made to fit a guy.

This technology shouldn't be in their hands, but how could I get out of the building with it? I decided to just put the thing on under the lab coat. I've always been pretty invisible so I counted on making that work for me. I grabbed a bunch of papers and a pencil and tried to look like I belonged there.

The mantra that *I fit in and I'm invisible* kept repeating in my mind, like that would make it happen. Slipping out the door, I tried to act like I was supposed to be there. Truthfully, I was afraid I would be stopped at any moment.

Walking quietly down the long hallway, I looked into a few more doorways.   At the end of the corridor I noticed an empty workshop.   My eye was drawn to something sitting on a worktable that looked suspiciously like a battery or power-pack.   It might be the power source for those buttons.   I took the power-pack, stuffed it into a pocket of my lab coat, and quietly left the workroom.

Down the hallway, I searched for some quiet place so I could take a look at my pilfered loot without being caught.   Even a closet would do, I joked to myself.

Further down, the long corridor branched off to another, more dimly lit passageway.   That dark area seemed to indicate "don't go down there."   John would probably know that's exactly what I would do!   I needed to find someplace unoccupied where I wouldn't be disturbed.   If this was an area they went out of their way to make people avoid, that would work for me.

As I bustled along, I passed a few other people.   I made it a point to just nod to them and seem as busy as they were.   They stayed occupied with their own errands, just nodding back and continuing on their way.   Ha!   Who needs blending techniques when you're invisible?

In the dark hallway, some rooms looked like they were best avoided.   People might notice a light on in a room that's supposed to be unlit.   I opened a door to one room which was dimly lit through a window along one interior wall.   At least I could see, though not very well.   Since there wasn't much else there, nobody should be using it any time soon.

A switch on the side of the wall activated more direct light. This was some sort of interrogation room, with a table and a few chairs.   It was the two-way mirror that allowed more light in from the observation room.   Both rooms were empty.

As I took off the lab coat and T.A.L.O.S. device, I looked for some indication as to where a power-pack should be attached. Inside the vest was a pocket with a flap covering some connectors, much like those for a nine-volt battery in a toy.

Should I turn it on?   I actually thought about not doing it. After all, it might short out and catch on fire.   Then no one would have it.   Of course, at the time I didn't stop to think that a fire might draw unwanted attention to me as I was being barbequed. Oh, well.   A decision had to be made.

I attached the power-pack and tucked it into the pocket. When I pressed a button accessible on the outer portion of the vest, nothing happened.   Randomly trying the others, I finally found what had to be the on button.   The thing seemed to come alive. Another made the vest go clear and become hard to distinguish from what was behind it.   That's why they want this technology!

Voices coming from down the hallway indicated I'd run out of time.   If people were coming to this area, that couldn't be good. I looked around quickly.   Where could I hide?

Then, it hit me.   Maybe, if I put this thing on, I might become invisible, too.   Translating thought into action, first, I put on the lab coat.   Then, I quickly shrugged into the vest.   At the last minute, I remembered the papers, and stuffed them into a lab coat pocket, hoping they would be hidden.

If they could see me, I'd die of embarrassment!   But there was no reflection in the two-way mirror, so I figured I'd be spared the mortification.

Waiting in a corner of the room, I tried to remain as quiet as possible.   A couple of mean-looking guys brought John in and roughly sat him down at the table.   They took a cursory look around the room.

What were they going to do to him?   At least he was alive and moving pretty much on his own.   The interrogations he'd already been through hadn't been too severe.   Some of his cuts and bruises looked fresh.   Now I understood what Vargas meant by a little worse for wear.

It wasn't a good idea to let John know I was there while the big bruisers were in the room, so I waited.

Then, Vargas walked in and sat down opposite him. Would the goons be told to use their skills to torture John?   Just how far could this double-agent be trusted?   He took the opportunity to look the bedraggled prisoner over a little and sent the goons to get his implements.   That sounded ominous, but it got the two underlings to leave immediately.

"I trust you were not roughed up too badly," Vargas said with a certain amount of compassion.

At that, John laughed a little, as much as a split lip would let him.   That must be a guy thing.

Then, Vargas stated, "Apparently, some of the technicians have misplaced the T.A.L.O.S. device.   I wonder what might have happened to it."

John jerked his head up at that question.   "Missing?" he asked.   He looked concerned.   "Do you think…?"

They both looked around, but the suave spy shook his head slightly to stop his friend's next words.   Vargas didn't seem to suspect that I was in the room.   At least he didn't let on that he knew there was someone else there with them.

"This stealth device could be used to smuggle drugs and arms.   The technology might even be enlarged and modified to conceal whole boxes of illegal cargo.   Even trucks or planes might be hidden.   We both know such a device, if it fell into the wrong hands, could be devastating.   It might be better to have it wind up missing than to leave it here."

"Yes, I agree," John said.

Well, well.   They and I were on the same page.   Such a stealth device could allow nefarious people and goods to get across a border.   It would even allow a person to be in a room with unsuspecting people, to listen in to their conversations, just like I was doing.

Vargas looked at John.   "You know what has to be done. Are you ready to continue?"

John hesitated, but nodded his head.

Vargas spoke in a quiet voice, "This could very well put Gia's life at stake.   Are you willing to do that?"

It chilled me to stand there and wait for John's answer.   He said nothing for a long while.   With a strained look on his face he finally answered, "Then she's just unfortunate collateral damage."

"So, you are telling me she is just an asset?"

I was surprised and appalled at those words.   John nodded, though he looked unhappy to admit it.   I had to keep myself from blurting out my indignation at being called an asset.   Despite my disbelief, I worked hard to calm my anger and keep my breathing even so I wouldn't give myself away.

At that point, the goons returned with a tray of various wicked-looking knives and a container of something else that was covered. They made a big show of laying the blades out so John could see them, and know what was coming. Nice.

Vargas turned to them. "You can go," he told them with authority.

One left, but the other man stood by the door.

Vargas raised an eyebrow at that show of disobedience.

The defiant guard gave a nasty smile and said, "Orders from higher up." The thug crossed his arms and continued to stand there by the doorway, eying both men with disdain.

Vargas stared at him for a moment, and turned in John's direction. He fingered one of the wicked-looking knives. When he said, "I am sorry, my friend, to have to do this," I really thought he was going to kill John. He picked up the knife and quickly turned toward the guard. He mercilessly raked the thin, flexible blade across the unsuspecting goon's neck and down his torso in two expert moves. The disobedient thug gurgled and fell to the floor in a puddle of blood.

At the sight, I had to clasp my hands across my mouth to stay quiet. At least it wasn't John's death I was forced to watch.

Vargas moved quickly to retrieve the gun from the dead man's body. He came back over to cut John's bonds. "The computer virus has been activated to infect the system. It will delete the stored data and disrupt the camera feed. Count to five, then go quickly, my friend." At least he was on our side, for now.

John rubbed his wrists where they had been bound, and told Vargas, "I'm not leaving without Gia." That statement made me feel better, although I recalled Vargas' words that John could never be totally truthful with me.

Vargas smiled and said "She is here."

Now, how did he know that? He hadn't acknowledged me, and John hadn't seemed to notice my presence, either. I glanced over into the mirror, and couldn't see myself, but I figured if Vargas knew, there was no sense in using up the power-pack unnecessarily.

As I turned off the T.A.L.O.S., I stated to John, "Worrying about you will be the death of me yet."

That startled him!   He wanted to say something, but I was quicker.   Being careful of his split lip, I leaned over and very lightly kissed him.   He was quite surprised.   Vargas seemed intrigued by the whole display.

After a brief moment to enjoy the kiss, I had to ask Vargas, "John didn't seem to notice me.   How did you know I was hiding in the room?"

He just gave me an enigmatic little smile and said, "I always know when a beautiful woman is near, my dear."

John raised an eyebrow at that.   To cover his interest he asked, "What about the escape plan?"

Their attention immediately got diverted to devising a plan. "Will it work to use the stealth capabilities of the T.A.L.O.S. vest to leave the compound unseen?" John asked.

Vargas nodded agreement.   "Gia has given us proof that it is functional enough to do the job.   I will provide some distraction for you two to leave, and we will all meet at the estate."   Before bursting through the door, he turned to John and said, "You will owe me big time, my friend."   He rushed out and immediately began firing the gun he'd taken, yelling, "The prisoner has escaped! He went around the corner.   Go get him!"

Putting the vest on John, I moved closer to ask, "How will the device work for a taller person?"

He adjusted it on his weary shoulders and said, "There's a dial somewhere.   Turn it up and the field will be increased."

As I did so, I took a brief glance in the mirror to see that he had disappeared.

"Keep your hand on my back," I told him.   That way, I'd know where he was at all times.   We ran from the interrogation room together.

"We should probably be quick.   Vargas can't stay there and dodge bullets forever," John whispered in my ear.

"I understand.   I don't know how long the power pack will last, either," I said, looking around.   "OK, this way," I whispered.

I vaguely remembered going down the dingy hallway, so we traveled back to the brighter-lit hallway, away from the sounds of gunfire.

John began leaning on me more heavily. He was in pain, and I didn't know how much more he could take. I became afraid that he might collapse before we got outside the building.

Guards came running down the hallway toward us. I was concerned they might run into John, but as I slowed, John stayed behind me. They ran past without paying me much attention. "This thing must work pretty well," I whispered to John when they had passed.

Vargas' computer virus had done what it was supposed to do. Roaming security personnel were everywhere, but they were looking for an intruder they could see. The suave spy himself had created enough chaos for us to leave undetected. I sincerely hoped that he wouldn't be hurt or killed in helping us to get away.

Passing into the atrium, we went by the security checkpoint where I had been given my identification badge. I thought about leaving it on the desk, but my years as a federal employee had instilled in me the aversion to losing my I.D. With all the computer information having been deleted by the virus, they wouldn't know about Hepsiba, so I didn't want to leave any clues. As we left the building and got to the parking lot, I pocketed the card.

Once we made it to the cars, the vest seemed to lose power. John was no longer invisible. Battery life and field strength were probably two of the problems the bad guys had been trying to solve.

John turned the device off. He wearily slumped down between Vargas' car and another one so we could hide. He was physically spent, but he motioned for me to pay attention to him.

"We need to take suspicion off of Vargas, and make sure he has transportation. Let's take this other one." Breathing heavily, John motioned to the car parked beside Vargas'. He was hurting and exhausted, but he got it hotwired quickly. He wanted to drive, of course.

"With your injuries and fatigue, you probably shouldn't do that. Besides, I know the route back to Vargas' villa. Trust me." I've been hanging around with Vargas too much! Well, OK, I turned left one time when I should have turned right. I joked, "I'm throwing off any pursuers this way." Fortunately, the poor guy was too tired to smirk too much at that.

Vargas, on the other hand, returned to his estate about the same time we did.   Thankfully, he never asked about what held us up.   I didn't volunteer any information about getting lost.   I whispered to John, "That side trip is strictly need-to-know!"   He just gave me a deadpan look, but didn't say a word.

We entered the villa through a side entrance, which I hadn't learned about in my snooping.   That area looked more utilitarian. It had concrete floors and walls instead of inlaid tiles and Persian rugs.

We went as quickly as we could down the drab hall to a stairwell.   One set of steps went up, but we continued down to a room with a mirror.

"This must be the observation area on the other side of the interrogation room," I said.

Vargas didn't say.   He quietly motioned us to sit at an institutional-looking metal table and spoke in hushed, hurried tones.   "The story I gave the Ravens Eye bosses was that people had been shooting at you while you were escaping.   Those employees who were killed were either collateral damage, or shot by you.   The implanted virus will delete all the surveillance footage, so there will be no proof.   I should be able to get away with it, at least for now."

John took off the heavy, fashion-backward vest and laid it on the table.   I put it in my lap for a bit.   While playing with it, I fingered the fastenings of the power-pack loose and tucked it in my pocket.   Then, I innocently put the vest back on the tabletop.

As John reached for it, he asked Vargas, "How long till your virus has deleted any of the information they reverse-engineered from the T.A.L.O.S.?"

Vargas considered the question.   "Once it spreads, it will delete everything from the computer.   However, there may still be some data stored on peripheral devices.   They will need to be plugged in for the virus to be uploaded.   I will check on it to make sure."   He actually looked concerned, and said, "It might take me at least 24 hours to get that information.   I will deal with it.   For now, there is a little room to the side.   It has a narrow bed and a tiny washroom where you can rest and wash up."   Vargas said apologetically, "It is better if the estate staff do not see you."

"I agree," John said in understanding. "I think I'll go clean up and rest." He set the vest back on the table. Once he was comfortable in the little side room, the door was closed.

Vargas and I were left alone in the outer room. He sat with me at the metal table. I fingered the vest thoughtfully.

Vargas asked, "Would you like to go upstairs to your room, or would you prefer to stay with John?"

My fingers kept playing with the vest as I thought about that question. I answered, "It might be better if your staff didn't see me, either. I'll stay here in case John needs me."

He thought about that, and gave a nod in agreement. "By the way, your techniques are quite unique. Some of your actions are what would be expected; while others seem... forgive me my dear... unusual and almost untrained. Where did you receive your training? It is so different that I must presume it was not from Langley."

I gawked at him for a moment. "What training?"

Vargas seemed rather embarrassed at his assumption. "I suspected you were some information analyst, at least! You were telling the truth? You are not some sort of agent working with John? I thought surely you were a liaison from some other agency, working under deep cover."

I shook my head. "I've provided information when I could, but he might not say I actually work *with* him. There have even been a few times when he's gotten a bit exasperated with me."

He thought for a moment and inclined his head toward me. "Well, I recognize your potential, my dear. Something John seems to have overlooked."

That made me smile.

Vargas thought some more. "The implanted virus will slow Ravens Eye down, but only temporarily. Eventually they will start searching for information on Velma and Hepsiba. Until then, your recent exploits will go unknown for a while."

"That's probably a good thing. If you can tap into Ravens Eye Group video feeds, could they tap into yours?" I asked.

"I assume they already have. The video in this area of my internal security has been put on a loop so no one will see that you came back here." Vargas nodded and turned to leave.

Before he closed the door I called, "Wait," to him.

He came back into the room.

I worked up my courage to ask, "What is going to become of this device?"

He thought about it and said, "John should probably take it to his people. If Ravens Eye Group catches me with it, they will undoubtedly kill me, most unpleasantly." What those information terrorists would do to someone who stole from them wouldn't be pretty. I certainly didn't want to be caught by them!

"How could John get it to his people without Ravens Eye Group knowing?"

Vargas thought and said, "I am not allowed to know about all aspects of his organization, but he will find a way." He turned to leave the concrete surveillance rooms. He was probably going to sleep in a luxurious bed upstairs.

I stayed downstairs, sitting in one of the metal chairs. I placed the other metal chair in front of the one I was using and tried to get comfortable. Sighing, I removed the wig and contacts. I propped my legs up and leaned back. It would have to do.

Despite the discomfort, I eventually drifted off into a light sleep. John quietly came out of the side room and awakened me. "If you want, you can come with me and get out of here. Why didn't you go upstairs? You could have been more comfortable." The look in his eyes told me that there was greater importance to that question than the mere words.

That woke me up. Giving him a glare, I told him, "You know better than that." His question was disturbing. I stopped to ask him, "What's with calling me an asset?"

He looked a little sheepish and said, "Never give up any information. You never know if it might be used against you."

That assuaged my mood. "We'll go together, or nothing." Stopping to give him a quick, hard kiss to make my point, I grabbed the vest to leave. The relieved look in his eyes when he learned I wanted to go with him further placated me. I gave him a nod as we walked out, satisfied that he thoroughly understood my meaning.

We looked out the metal door for security cameras, but didn't see any. I whispered, "I hadn't seen this stairwell on the monitors when I was in Vargas' security control room. He also told me that the security footage was on a loop, so we shouldn't be seen as we leave."

He nodded, and we made our way up the stairs to get out of the building. He said quietly, "Opening the door might set off an alarm, so we'd better hurry." We hustled over to the car we'd used to get to Vargas' estate. Fortunately, it was fairly quiet and had enough gas to get us away from the mansion. Despite still being in rough shape, he insisted on driving.

On the way out, I asked him why we were sneaking away.

He cryptically said, "Vargas can't tell what he doesn't know." That made sense. Vargas hadn't been seen leaving the stronghold with the vest. What Ravens Eye Group didn't know hopefully wouldn't get him in trouble.

John borrowed my phone and made a few calls. Then, we pulled out in the stolen vehicle. We both were quiet as he drove.

My head started nodding just as John pulled off the road. Another vehicle was already parked there.

He got out and Agent Smith sauntered up.

Stepping out of the car, I walked around a little to wake up while John and Smith conferred about the situation.

I heard her ask, "Are you OK?"

"I'll live," he replied, though he looked like he was running on fumes.

"This is just great. I'm reduced to being 'an asset,' while Agent Smith gets to come and save the day," I mumbled out of earshot.

John came over, took the vest from me, and handed it to Agent Smith.

After securing the device in a case in the other vehicle, she returned and asked me, "How are you doing?"

All I could manage was a nod. I felt physically and emotionally drained. The adrenaline rush of everything I'd been through had worn off, so I didn't go into any detail with her.

She was off in a flash before I could even think of anything to say, anyway.

John came back over. He did show some concern as he looked me over quickly and asked, "Are you OK?"

I mumbled something in the affirmative.

He shook his head in wry humor and told me, "I think I've aged ten years in the time I've known you." He gave a tired sigh. "There will be another vehicle here shortly. It will take you to the airport."

Sure enough, another car pulled up right then. "So, it's to be the same type of thing. You go off and I get sent home." After what we'd been through I was so tired and cranky, but something about being sent away again after what we'd accomplished seemed anticlimactic and unfair.

I turned toward the waiting vehicle, and he gave an "ahem." I reluctantly shifted back to see what he wanted.

He stepped up to me and asked in a low voice, "Aren't you forgetting something?"

"As exhausted as I am, I wouldn't be surprised to find I've forgotten my own name," I said grumpily.

The look in his eyes told me what he meant, although I tried to ignore it. Were his feelings real, or was this just something used to keep an "asset" coming back for more? It would have been so nice to have given in to his magnetism.

At that point I was too weary to face the larger implications of this relationship. I knew I'd make myself crazy thinking about what it was and whether it was real or just my imagination. Part of me yearned to feel his arms around me, but my hands hung down to my pockets. Then, I felt something there. Had John been talking about us or the stupid power-pack?

With an unhappy look at John, I reached in my pocket and retrieved the item. "Yes, I almost forgot this," and I handed it to him, perhaps a little too forcefully.

John looked surprised, but just then Agent Smith came back up to him with some urgent business. While the two of them were preoccupied, I quietly said, "I guess I'll see you later." I walked over to the waiting sedan that would start me on my journey home.

The trip to the airport was quiet. I wasn't in the mood for conversation, anyway. Along the way, I thought about the things John and I had done and what we'd shared. Wiping the tears from my eyes, I hoped the driver was concentrating on the road and wasn't paying attention to me.

***

When I got out at passenger loading, the driver took the false I.D. from me and admonished me to never mention the fake names again. That was fine with me. I took the tickets and documents the driver had given me to get me home.

The airport terminal was crowded and noisy, even for that early in the morning. By that time, I was too tired and upset to even look around the area. I was sad that I hadn't even gotten to say goodbye. "Another packed flight," I said unhappily, judging from the throng of people waiting to board the plane. I was about as miserable and cranky as the other people around me seemed to be.

Physically, I was exhausted, but my mind kept racing. I thought about John and was alternately angry and distraught. Was I just someone who assisted him, an asset that he used when needed, or his girlfriend? What did I want out of this relationship? Did I have the right to assume anything further? What was John expecting out of it? Was I just another job to him? I knew it would be a long flight home, but what would happen after that? What would become of this feeling was that was growing between us? I had no answers.

They eventually called for general boarding. I showed my ticket, found my seat, and plopped myself down. "Great! I get to fly for hours, crammed in a small coach seat, and they have to put me in the middle! Couldn't they at least have gotten me a window seat?" Yes, by that time I was grousing to the universe.

There was some unknown delay, but finally the plane pulled away from the gate and got airborne. We were on our way, but in my sour mood, I couldn't have cared less. I couldn't tell if I was hungry, or thirsty, or upset.

Chapter 12

My brain hurt, my stomach was unsettled, and my heart was aching. Leaning back in the cramped, uncomfortable coach seat, I closed my eyes. The noisy cabin and narrow seat didn't allow for much relaxation, though.

My thoughts wandered back to John for about the millionth time. What are we to each other? Will our relationship ever reach a level of confidence where these things aren't an insurmountable obstacle? What happens if it doesn't? What would I do? Was this what Vargas was trying to tell me?

The plane reached altitude and people started talking and walking around the cabin. At that point, someone asked to switch places with the person sitting in the aisle seat next to me. The passenger helpfully gave up his seat. That jostled me out of my deep thoughts, and I looked over at the person settling into the seat beside me.

It was John! I didn't know what to think, but a glimmer of hope started to grow. The discolorations around his face and chin had deepened, and he had dark circles under his eyes to rival his bruises. It was obvious he was sore and tired. He gave me a look that made me melt, and my expression softened.

I asked, "Are you the reason for the delay in pulling out?" He just gave his usual half-grin and tentatively tried to make some conversation with me. "So, was this your first trip to Sedona?"

My narrowed eyes indicated my bad mood. "You should know it was."

Recognizing my unhappy state, he tried again. "I know that look. We've both been through a lot. Let's see if we can't achieve some kind of understanding. I know more about you than you do about me. How about we make plans to fix that?"

I was half-crazed with fatigue and worry and, yes, a bit of anger. However, I could tell he was allowing me into his life more than ever before. Here he was, on the flight with me, talking with me instead of dealing with who-knows-whatever else he still had to face. Grudgingly, I had to concede that this was, perhaps, his quiet way of showing me that he was grateful for his rescue. He *had* been beaten up and I *had* come to his aid, with Vargas' help.

"How much of this offer is out of gratitude, and how much is really relating to feelings for me?" I challenged. "That may sound shrewish, but I have to know." Desolately, I looked away and leafed through a travel magazine from the seat-back in front of me.

"Let's see," he said. He took the magazine, which had a tropical scene on the cover and offered, "How about we go to someplace like that beach so we can really talk?"

He was trying his best. I knew it, but I had to say, "You know, I can't figure out what I am to you, and it worries me. Am I just an asset?"

He at least had the honesty to look a little bit guilty at that.

I glared at him. "I really need to know. It wasn't exactly flattering. We've never really discussed what we are to each other, what our relationship is, it's true. I realize that we're still getting to know each other..." I tried to continue. "I lo–," but I chickened out and didn't use the word *love*. I cleared my throat and changed it to, "I'd be lost without you, but if we don't straighten this out, the potential for pain is too great."

It didn't come out the way I felt inside. The uncertainty of the situation made me want to avoid the bitter potential of rejection and failure. It was easier to hide behind the excuse that I'd been away from work too long, and more time off wouldn't be accepted. I kept that to myself because I knew too well that my dull job was simply a means to keep a roof over my head. Deep down, I just had to find out where this might lead.

He could tell I was hurt and unsure about his vacation idea. "Let me try to soothe some of your bruised feelings." He leaned over to me. "We can see if I can answer some of your questions. I can see you'd like to. Come on. No guns, bombs, or bullets; just a real vacation," he promised. "Besides, it'll take about a month to get things sorted out. The agency is going to want a piece of me for this. That's for sure."

John saw my concern about that, but he reassured me with his cocky grin, "Don't worry. The successful acquisition of that device will smooth things over." Then he said, "You're probably going to need some time to yourself, anyway."

That startled me, and I had to ask, "Why is that?"

He shrugged and said "Post-mission decompression. Most first-timers normally need time to process what went on during an assignment, and you haven't actually had all the training." He looked at me with admiration, "Although you did pretty well, considering."

He leaned closer and whispered, "Some NSA people will be meeting us at the airport to ask some questions. Just be yourself and answer truthfully. It's all part of procedure, but it won't be anything you can't handle. Debriefings aren't any fun and you'll probably hold some of that against me for a few days."

"Now you tell me? I was scared trying to rescue you, but this sounds terrifying. I'm not sure I have the strength or desire to go through a debriefing."

This news was a real eye-opener! I had interpreted John's dealing with people, such as Agent Smith, as working around me. Now I could see the actions as perhaps shielding me from certain parts of his job and protecting me from aspects of his dangerous life. With this, he was letting me in. All the way in.

Yes, I know how that sounds! It's one thing to flirt with a mysterious man. It's a different situation altogether to step beyond that veil of secrecy and see what really goes on.

This was what I wanted; to be allowed into his world and have a closer relationship with him. Would this alter things, and change *us*, forever? I had misgivings that I was ready to accept whatever might happen. We quietly talked of vacation plans and spoke about our likes and dislikes and hopes for the future.

He told me, "I went to an Ivy League college and then joined the military. I enjoy outdoor activities and sports. I've lost people I've cared about. I've witnessed people used and betrayed, and that has bothered me."

"Since the incident with Arty, I've been more opposed to bullies and manipulators. I'm concerned with all the many laws I must have broken. Are they going to throw the book at me and take me to jail?" I fretted, unsure how bad this meeting at the airport was going to be.

He assured me that I wasn't in trouble. "They'll just ask some questions and make you sign a nondisclosure agreement."

"That probably means I'm still not considered one of you, which may, or may not, be a good thing." After that, I reached my emotional limit. In exhaustion, I wound up falling asleep with my head on John's shoulder as he made soothing circles on my neck with his fingers. Dreams of what this interrogation would entail played in my subconscious. The fear that I didn't want to find out what they might do to people who fail these debriefings kept repeating itself through my nightmare.

***

We finally landed in Seattle. Since I'd been sent home without my luggage, there was nothing to pick up. At least we didn't have to spend time waiting at baggage claim.

John and I were met by a group of people as we came out of the gate area. Two men in security uniforms and a couple women in dark suits came up to us. They all looked very serious and scary.

I confided to John, "They seem so... stone-cold deadly." I don't know if they heard me, but the agents positioned themselves around us and we were given a "perp walk" through the airport. I was mortified.

"People are watching us while trying not to make it obvious that they're watching. It's humiliating," I complained quietly to John under the baleful glare of our security guards.

John put his arm around me and said, "Just smile. People will make of it what they want, and then their attention moves on to other things. Remember, the public doesn't need to be aware of some things."

We were escorted to some conference rooms in a TSA area. John gave my hand a quick squeeze as he was led by the suited female agents into one meeting room. The other two uniformed officials ushered me to another one. I was instructed to sit down at the table. A nice young lady introduced herself as a polygraph

examiner and put sensors on me. They were attached to a lie
detector machine. She asked me a lot of questions.

"Tell me about the previous places where you've lived."
Next she asked, "Where have you worked in the last ten years?"
Those questions touched upon every aspect of my life. "Who have
your most recent friends, associates and co-workers been?" It was
probably to see if I'd mess up. They were familiar questions, since
I've been through background security checks before.

The officials asked me why I had done what I did. I stated,
"I have a strong sense of loyalty and civic duty. I wanted to help
John, even though I wasn't trained." I admitted, "Purpose matters
to me, and trustworthiness is important. It's not like there has
been very much of that in my regular job, as I told you. Vargas
even told me to be wary of my boss."

That statement led them to ask me about Vargas, but there
was only so much I could tell them. "Vargas had alerted me to
certain things, and helped me in John's rescue." That was the
truth.

They asked, "Why didn't you bring it to the authorities?
They would have handled it." It sounded like they were surprised
I handled the job myself. More like they didn't expect that I *could*
do the job, even with Vargas' help!

"When I heard that John was in trouble, I didn't know who
to call. This isn't exactly an ordinary situation. Vargas'
information was quite convincing. He told me time was critical.
I must act immediately or John would die. He also said to be
careful who I told. I didn't know who I could trust. There was no
time to try to find someone who'd believe me, anyway." When I
told them that, I gave them both a steely look. They probably
didn't like that comment.

Then they got into some questions about John. I had no
guideline for this, since I'd never been through a debriefing before.
The interrogators asked, "So you were convinced to do this all by
yourself?" I recalled what Vargas had told me. "There was some
mistake as to whether I might be some sort of agent or information
analyst or something. It also could have been that whoever Vargas
works for didn't want to expend their resources and blow his cover,
which makes sense."

They double-checked that I had turned in Velma Antwerp's I.D. documents. At that point, I'd had enough. "Look, I've been through a lot recently. I did what I had to do to get John rescued, yet none of you seem to be at all grateful." I crossed my arms at delivering that statement. After that they decided to close the questioning.

The stack of secrecy papers they laid in front of me to sign was enormous. I'm used to bureaucracy, but the size of that pile blew me away. Of course, I get the point that having the bad guys out there, especially when one isn't supposed to know they exist, is a bad thing. Interfering with the ones who are trying to stop that threat is even worse. Becoming aware of the danger has changed my perspective.

That debriefing clarified things in my mind and made it easier for me to understand John's motivations. Someone in his line of work has to maintain some principles and keep a sense of purpose, despite shifting policies and politics. That's a very fine line to walk every day. It's a stark fact that someone like John is really out there alone, working without much of a safety net.

About two grueling hours after I had entered that room, they let me go. They gave me a stern reminder about not ever divulging anything. "Who's going to believe me?" I retorted. Maybe I was pushing my luck a little bit, but I really wanted to be done with them. By that point, I was grouchy and tired. My mind whirled as I trudged out to the taxi ramp just outside the airport terminal.

John walked up to me. As exhausted as I was, I was also keyed up from the debriefing, and in no mood for conversation. He stayed close while we were waiting for our respective cabs, but he was his usual quiet self. Smart man.

After a bit, I couldn't take it anymore. I turned to him and said accusingly, "Do you know that the debriefing team asked me questions about you?"

He just looked at me calmly and said, "I'm not surprised at all. I'd be more surprised if they hadn't asked any. It's all just standard procedure."

"I don't understand how you can take it so calmly!" When he started to say something, I held my hand up to stop him. I was pretty irritable and said, "I need to get myself together before we talk. This has been one hell of a day! You had mentioned it would take a while to complete your reports. So, go kill a forest for all your paperwork, make sixteen different copies of your documents for filing, and satisfy whatever bureaucracy you need to placate on your end." Yes, I made bureaucracy sound like a dirty word.

He smiled at me and said, "You do get cranky sometimes." He leaned in close and whispered, "That's how I know when you're worrying about me."

That was about the time when the taxies arrived. He pulled me in to hold me tight and gave me a quick but meaningful kiss.

All I could do was put my arms around him. His strong presence emboldened me. We both put everything in that kiss. "I can't tell if I'm steaming mad or sizzling with desire," I whispered to him when we came up for breath.

He just smiled at me and said, "Wow." His taxi honked and he hurriedly said, "I'll miss you." He headed off.

I shook my head and grinned as I walked over to my taxi. I sincerely hoped that the next time we met would be the good kind of "hot."

Chapter 13

John left to decimate a forest to complete his paperwork, and I caught a taxi back home. It had only been a few days since I had left to rescue him, but I certainly wasn't the same person I had been before I made the trip. With the experiences I had gained and the modification this journey had forced in my outlook, I was a changed person. What I wanted out of life, and knew I could accomplish, were expanded.

Walking through the front door of my apartment, I threw my keys on the kitchen table. Glancing over, I checked for any messages. I noticed there were a few. "It doesn't matter. Those can wait till tomorrow." I knew they were just something from my old, boring life. That life didn't suit me anymore. I had a lot of serious decisions to contemplate concerning what I wanted for my future, and I really didn't want to waste any further time on trivial, mundane things.

My perspective had changed about the job and my abilities. Beyond that, there was the riddle of my relationship with John. We were good together. I knew that. I felt we could be great together. After all, if I could fly to Arizona to successfully rescue him from the clutches of techno-terrorists, then this feeling had to be explored. This may just be infatuation or an insane need to put myself in danger, but I was going to see to it that we took advantage of this opportunity. Who knew? Maybe I could even find a more satisfying job.

In a tired daze, I threw on some pajamas and went to bed. Would a relationship with John work? What did Vargas really want, and was he really out of the picture? Those questions plagued me as I tossed and turned. The way those two interacted, they had to be on the same side. Why hadn't I seen it sooner? Should John have said something? Did I want to go back to my boring job? Could I find anything better? Should I buy some more Rocky Road ice cream?

Around and around my thoughts churned. After a lot of tossing and turning, I finally fell into a fitful sleep. Distorted dreams played in my mind, where job searches and debriefings and people with deceptive agendas trying to keep me from getting my Rocky Road ice cream home all merged together.

The doorbell jarred me awake. I spared a quick look at the time, and couldn't believe it was almost 10 AM. I hastily donned a robe and answered the door.

It was a delivery guy, asking me to sign for a package. I asked to see who it was from before I signed for it. After what I'd been through, I wasn't taking any chances, although I didn't dare tell him that!

He mumbled, "Why can't you just sign the receipt?" As I handed the paperwork back to him, I gave the impatient guy the steely-eyed look I've been perfecting and told him, "Trust me, you don't want to know!" That remark made him leave quickly!

The box was from Vargas. Why would he overnight me something? I was still shaking my head when I opened the box. In it was my carryon case with my clothes. Among my things was that evening dress I had worn my first night at his villa. That was surprising. He had written a note: "I can no longer picture anyone else in this gown. It is truly meant for you."

"Vargas, you really are a romantic," I laughed to myself. The appearance of the suitcase confirmed my suspicions that Vargas wasn't totally out of the picture.

Since I was up, I decided to start some coffee brewing and have a quick breakfast. As I was waiting for my coffee, I decided maybe I'd listen to the messages I'd ignored the previous night.

Some group had called. "We would like you to participate in a telephone survey." The next was a message from the dentist's office: "We want to remind you that it's time to come in for a cleaning." I deleted both of those. Then, some friends had called me. "Hey, Gia, we're going out and we want to know if you'd like to come with us tonight." That had happened a couple nights ago. I made a mental note to ask them how things had gone.

The last message was from my boss. "Ah, Gia, I need to know where the information to make the monthly report is found." It hadn't escaped my notice that he had figured I'd be at home.

I groused to the phone, "You still can't manage that simple task by yourself, after all this time."

The person I'd become was no longer satisfied with this life. If I could tell my friends about my transformation, they might not believe me. I knew better than to say anything because I wanted to keep them out of trouble. What I'd experienced was hard enough. I wouldn't inflict the unpleasant details on my friends. Something I never figured I'd need to say, but it was also a matter of national security.

Could I balance my desire for more challenge with the need for survival? Evaluating the pros and cons weighed on me for the rest of my time off. Should I allow myself to be dragged back into that boring but safe routine, or risk everything by asking to be moved somewhere else potentially more fulfilling?

***

The routine at work irritated more than it had before. "Gee, there are always problems with the copier, or some report. If it isn't that, it's with some computer hardware, or software," I complained to myself.

Along with the work problems, my thoughts kept returning to John and how he was doing. What would a future together be like? I could anticipate that it would be days, or even weeks, of loneliness when he went off and did what he needed to do. If he didn't come home when expected, I would be filled with terrified worry. When he did come home, what then? His work gave him day-to-day variety, while I had a mundane, routine job. Would I get a little boring to be around after a while? How would I feel about being kept on the outside?

Despite the knowledge that there would be a lot of problems to overcome, I knew I couldn't leave him to face things all alone. However, it took an extremely brutal day at work to force me to come to a decision about this job. First the boss couldn't make up his mind. Once he decided what he wanted, he became unhappy because I couldn't seem to deliver it quickly enough. I was forced to realize that this job could never challenge my new capabilities. I needed more fulfillment and excitement than this.

Before leaving work that very day, I made up my mind. I also remembered what Vargas had told me about not trusting my boss. That added to my determination to speak to the people who had placed me here.

***

Finally, the workday ground to a close. "I can't wait to get home and put on some sweats and get comfortable," I said to myself at the end of that grueling day. I also needed to come to terms with this new decision. A couple times, I dialed and hung up. On the third try I let it ring and talked to the people who had assigned me to this job. During the phone call, I spoke up about what Vargas had told me concerning this boss.

At first they were a little incredulous. They assured me they'd check things out and do what they could.

The doorbell rang just as I was settling in with a cup of tea and a book. Through the peephole, I saw a very haggard-looking John standing there. Unlocking the door quickly, I invited him in.

"You look tired. I had expected you to be rested after these weeks."

He clearly was not.

"Come on in. Sit down. Could I make you some coffee? Perhaps some tea would be better, or maybe something stronger? At least the bruises have faded," I said, giving his face a quick look and running my fingers where they had been.

"Some tea would be nice," he said. The poor guy looked weary. Instead of sitting on the couch, he followed me to the kitchen. He grabbed my hand and pulled me into a tight embrace. He whispered, "Work has been demanding, but I've been sleepless thinking about the two of us."

His words gave me some hope after the desolate weeks I'd spent. I put my arms around him and held him tightly, letting his warmth seep into me. "I'm glad that you were thinking about me. I've been thinking about you, too."

For a long moment, we just stood there, holding on to each other. Then, I released him and motioned for him to sit at the table. I sat down next to him and told him, "We need to talk."

He looked anxious. His mouth formed a tense line and he said, "Is this where you tell me you can't take my line of work and I need to hit the road?"

That spoke volumes about his life. It was probably hard for him to maintain a relationship with his kind of job.

I immediately told him, "No, not that kind of talk, but I need to know where we're headed. I just want some assurance that this is going to be long term. And I want to be more than an asset."

He sat there for a while looking at me. With his unreadable expression, I couldn't tell if he was angry or if he was thinking of telling me to take a hike! His silence was hard to bear.

I looked down at my hands. "I can't stand the uncertainty anymore. Throw me a lifeline. Please?" I was sad and almost to tears at that point.

Maybe he wanted to get a little payback because I left him so abruptly in Sedona. Maybe he was just searching for the words. I still don't fully understand what's going on in his complicated mind. He leaned over and gave me a long, firm, breathtaking kiss. It was serious and sincere. It was one of those kisses that went far beyond words.

"Does that tell you what you need to know?" he whispered intensely when we finally broke the kiss.

Finding my voice was difficult, but I smiled and told him, "Yes, for now, at least." I took his hand and led him down the hall to the bedroom. Our two hands fit together perfectly as his warm fingers caressed mine. We closed the door on the external issues for a while and started working on the interpersonal ones. Soon, we were rediscovering how well we fit together in other ways, too.

Chapter 14

After that, John no longer had to "prove" I was more than an asset. He had made it clear that we were working toward a future together and that satisfied me. We started spending more time with each other. Things began to change dramatically.

He encouraged me to enroll in a self-defense class and some handgun training for my protection. On a few occasions, he took me along to the firing range for practice. We went in to the section of the range where they rent guns and I pointed to one, "I'd like to try that one."

He gave me a look, like he wanted to say something. He probably wanted to tell me to try a smaller gun, but I was adamant. We picked up the paper targets and moved to the range to set up.

He fired first. Then I fired, doing my best. At least I kept the bullets within the outer rings of the target, so I was happy. He just looked at me and said, "Nice, tight grouping. Good job."

Toying with him, I fluttered my eyelashes and said, "Bullets or derriere?" Of course, then his eyes were drawn to my rear.

The repressed person I was had been replaced with a very mischievous woman and I had to give him a kiss right there! Some of his buddies started whistling and making comments, but we just ignored it.

At work, I was moved to another building. I never saw the previous boss again, so I have no idea what happened to him. The on-line security training kept me occupied. I also signed up for whatever else I thought I might get away with studying. I learned lots of things, except online parachute training! Ha!

To pass some lonely evenings, I even found a book that showed how spies use disguises and techniques to hide. All that contributed to my empowerment.

My wardrobe evolved from the bland and frumpy items to more colorful and fashionable clothes. My attitude had also begun to get bolder. I could feel the differences these changes made, though I'm still not totally comfortable with the transformation. Due to some of the training I was receiving, I had even come to appreciate Agent Smith. She told me at one point that she's out front so she can protect the team members behind her. The way she put it was, "That's an important part of my job." That definitely gave me a different perspective. Shortly after that, she had even taken a bullet while working with John. She had a bulletproof vest on, but still, that earned her some admiration from me.

***

Eventually, it was time for me to answer the grand jury's questions. Fortunately, because the crimes had been committed all across the country, I wasn't required to fly back to where I'd first encountered the nefarious Ravens Eye. I could give my deposition where I'd been reassigned.

The night before I was to testify, John stayed by my side to keep me safe. It was probably also to make sure I didn't stress out too much. We stayed in, and he helped me cook a meal, complete with candles and wine. The anxiety of the next day's testimony dulled my appetite a bit and I couldn't enjoy the food.

"I know just what you need." He led me to the bedroom. We didn't even clear the dinner dishes in our haste.

We kept each other occupied most of the evening. The next morning, we dragged ourselves out for the rendezvous with the protective detail. We may have been tired, but the stress we had felt the night before was as spent as the burned-out candles that had been forgotten on the table.

The security detail was silent and alert as they fell in around us. John assumed the agent-in-charge position behind and to my right, while Agent Smith took the position in front. Another two agents took positions behind John and me, to our left and right, forming a triangle along with Agent Smith. I had learned a little of protective details from nights scouring the internet waiting for John, but to see it in action was daunting.

An obscure, unmarked building was our destination. We got out and the agents again surrounded me. It was interesting how much safer I felt once we were actually in the elevator.

Once under oath, I was quizzed. They asked what seemed to be the same questions, but in different ways, to see if my answers matched. They wanted very exact information. It was exhausting. Neither the rigorously demanding lawyer who had been assigned to me, nor the endlessly probing questions of the jury, could intimidate me anymore. What I'd previously been through at the hands of Ravens Eye was much scarier.

After hours of testimony, I was drained. Even the lawyer assisting me was impressed with my answers. I was asked to wait for an hour, in case the jury had more questions.

***

With the examination over and my civic duty finally done, John made good on his promise about a real vacation. In between work and training, he and I had fun planning where we would go. While I didn't really expect it to happen, it was exciting to dream. "Take a look at this," I'd say, and show him brochures of exotic places like Tonga and Bora-Bora. We had a blast just figuring out all the exciting things we could do in those faraway places.

"The only problem is, the further away the place, the longer it will take to get there and back," John said. "Those exotic places leave us too little time for a vacation on my schedule."

We focused on places closer to home, but the Grand Canyon and theme parks just didn't seem to suit us, either.

One day, John said, "We could go to the Caribbean." He showed me some information and a timetable of available flights.

"The flight times seem to be acceptable, and we'll still have enough time to enjoy a decent vacation," I agreed. "Lots of sun, sand, surf, and umbrella drinks. I can do that!"

We coordinated our leave schedules and made the airline and hotel reservations. This would be my first real vacation with John and it filled me with nervous anticipation. I was hoping that the trip would move our relationship to the next level. John needed to take a breather from his hectic work schedule. It would also give me a much needed break from the day-to-day work and training I was taking.

"This flight is far more pleasant than the one from Sedona," I mentioned to John when we were in the air. "It's always more pleasant to be going toward something fun and positive than getting away from people torturing you or trying to kill us." I didn't know how prophetic those thoughts were going to turn out to be.

Customs was easy to get through because the airline lost my luggage. All I had was my big floppy hat, carry-on case, and the clothes I had worn.

There's always a price to be paid for something important. I wanted this significant next step in our relationship to go right. Unfortunately, it was to be without the sexy lingerie I had bought for John's enjoyment. I was disappointed, but I decided to save that information about what awaited him till my bag was found.

After we checked in at our hotel, I told him, "I'll just have to buy a few things till they locate my luggage."

It was still early enough, so we went out to make the purchases I required. The crowded streets and the exotic atmosphere provided a nice change from having to hide. "I don't want to drag you around all day with my shopping," I told him, so I bought a few essential items and we stopped at a café for something cool to drink.

After we were rested and rejuvenated, John suggested we might try walking down some of the smaller side streets to explore the area a bit.

We saw vendors selling all sorts of interesting and colorful things from carts. "It's so festive and fun," I enthused. That was when I spotted someone who looked suspiciously like Vargas. If he saw us, I was afraid our vacation would be ruined.

I quickly pulled John into a kiss to try to keep us from being seen. He almost stumbled on top of me, so it wasn't the most graceful maneuver, but was it ever hot! He was caught off guard but he didn't seem to mind!

After a bit, I looked around and didn't see the suspicious person. When I told John, "I thought I saw our mutual friend, Vargas," his smile quickly faded and he scanned the area.

"That doesn't mean we have to leave so soon, does it?" I was dismayed. We became more watchful and took a roundabout way back to our hotel. Neither of us saw anyone we recognized in the crowd. I tried to convince myself that it wasn't Vargas after all.

"We're both tired after the flight, so let's just stay in our room tonight," John suggested. After ordering room service, he had an idea. "How about we pick up where the kiss this afternoon left off? I don't like leaving unfinished business," he said, leaning into me. Oh! Those gorgeous eyes were dancing.

"Gee," I said mischievously to him, "Whatever shall I do with such a cocky man!" Soon we were both in bed, where he definitely showed me what could be done. The sultry Caribbean nights were nothing like the steam I felt with that man! I realized that he was the missing piece of my life. Without him, it would be very empty.

***

The next morning, John woke me with heated kisses and caresses. He closed his eyes and tilted his head back as he gave himself over to the sensation when I reached over and stroked his hair. It was gratifying to watch. Soon, he propped himself up on his arm to kiss me and he began to get more ardent with his attention. After that, we both needed to be sated. Soon, the two of us got lost in the shared feelings.

Later, as we were lying there, experiencing the aftershocks, I enjoyed the warmth and comfort of just being close to him. He rested close to me and his moist breath tickled my ear.

"You know, this is the best vacation I've had in a long time. In fact, this is about the only real vacation I've had in years. I'm so glad you're here to share it with me."

"You are a man who aims for my heart." I gave him a slow, meaningful kiss to show him how much being on vacation with him meant to me, too!

After more cuddling and further bonding, our stomachs were growling, so we got ready to go out for brunch. John got into some lightweight khaki pants and a polo shirt. I put on one of the airy dresses I had bought the day before. I briefly delighted in the difference I felt when I saw myself in something other than the usual drab office attire I used to wear. I was alive and in love. Life was good.

As we finished our food at the little sidewalk café, we were chatting over coffee when he told me, "Don't turn around."

I almost did, but stopped and asked, "What's the problem?"

He quietly told me, "You might have been right yesterday afternoon. It's possible that was Vargas you saw."

My floppy, wide-brimmed hat covered my head and face very well, and I was glad. I had originally brought it to protect me from the sun, but it was also the best camouflage I could come up with on the spur of the moment. Some of the things I learned as I was hiding out were being put to use in the field.

I moved to be between John and the person we thought was Vargas, thinking I'd give him some cover. John had a hard time trying to see around my hat.

"At least whoever it was wouldn't be able to see you so easily," I explained. I angled to the side a bit so he could see around the brim a little better. "I hope that our vacation won't be ruined if it does turn out to be him," I said.

"I can see him talking with some unknown man," John said quietly. "We'll leave the opposite direction."

On an impulse, I pulled John into a little clothing store on our way. I whispered to him, "You need to blend in." I picked out some surfer shorts and a garish tropical shirt for him to try on. I smirked, "You won't be recognized in shorts and an outrageous shirt!"

To his credit, he went along with my plan and tried them on. He came out to show me what my choices looked like together. His cocked eyebrow said it all.

"I have to get a picture of this!" I said, grinning.

He asked, "Why do you need to take a photo of me dressed like this?"

I laughed and said "You're just so cute with that expression on your face!"

He pulled me close and nuzzled my ear saying, "If this picture gets around to anybody, I'll never live it down and I'll have to shoot them." Then his lips twitched, and his eyes crinkled, so I knew he was teasing.

I ran my fingertip across his lips and relented, deleting the photo.

He bought different shorts and a more subdued shirt, telling me, "These clothes aren't so flashy." The sales clerk rang up the purchase, and even snipped the tags off so John could wear the outfit out of the store. Putting his other clothes in the bag, we ventured outside again.

In the next shop, I purchased a ball cap for John and a different hat for me. I put the old, floppy one in the bag. "That's about all they covered on changing and blending in. I just hope it'll be enough to keep us from being recognized," I said, satisfied with my work.

He smiled. "You must really want this vacation."

I admitted, "Of course I do. After all, we've both been looking forward to it for a while now."

We walked back to our hotel and had no more sightings of the elusive Vargas. We were tired and hot from our expedition. We unlocked the door to our hotel room. John took my hands and said, "Let's take a dip in the hotel pool to cool off." He had that look in his eyes that I just love.

As we were getting ready to do that, we found Vargas had left a message for us on the room's phone. "I was sure I had seen you two. I do hope you both are enjoying yourselves. Much as I dislike interrupting, I really need to meet with you two, perhaps at the little café downstairs at your hotel at 8 PM this evening?"

As the message ended I asked, "How did he know where we're staying? Why did he want to talk to both of us?" I was surprised to be included. We were equally intrigued, but we had no answers.

Not long before we were to meet with Vargas, John got an urgent call on his cell phone from Agent Smith. "Several new reports have come in. I wanted you to be aware that some killings have taken place down where you are. It's almost a purge within the Ravens Eye organization in the area. We've been able to verify that a number of the local members are known to be dead. The deaths are rumored to have been instigated by an insider.

We're still trying to get more information on that. I know you're on vacation, but I knew you'd want a heads up. You don't want to walk into something blind."

At that news, I asked, "Really? Was that insider Vargas? Or do you think that perhaps he is being targeted by someone in the organization and the others were just collateral damage?"

"I'm sure we'll find out tonight," John replied.

Chapter 15

We were curious as we went to the little café to meet with Vargas. When we sat down, Agent Smith was seated not far from our table. She was probably there to give John some backup.

John saw that I had noticed her and whispered to me, "Don't call attention to her."

I tried not to look at her, but I told John, "Someday you'll have to tell me her first name."

A waiter came by with some drinks for us, which prevented his answering the question. There was also a cell phone on the tray, which was handed to John. The server explained, "You apparently lost the phone and it is being returned to you."

John took it and thanked the waiter without looking too curious about it. The phone immediately rang. John mouthed that it was Vargas.

All I could hear was John's side of the conversation. He said, "Yes," a few times and hung up. John told me, "I'm texting Smith to go back and check the hotel rooms." We watched as she left immediately.

John led me in the opposite direction, which confused me. "Why is she sent one way while we're going another, when she was clearly supposed to give you backup?"

All he said was, "Just wait."

"OK. I can be patient," I told him. We went quickly down one crowded street to another, and then into one small back street to another. I asked John, "Aren't we going to meet Vargas?" I was thoroughly lost by the time we slowed down.

He just nodded and urged me on. We walked down a less-traveled byway when he noticed someone following us. My worry increased when he pulled me into a little shop. We passed through and quickly went out the back door. Fortunately, that put us right where we needed to be. We walked across the way into the little bar where we were to meet Vargas and saw him waiting for us. John returned the phone Vargas had used to contact us.

The suave spy had told me before that he was an enforcer for an information cartel, which I had later learned was Ravens Eye Group. However, his news was eye opening.

"I was sent to infiltrate Ravens Eye Group. My mission was to keep an eye on them and find out what they were planning."

"I'm glad to know you're really not a bad guy!" I told him.

He smiled, and continued, "To curtail their operations, I planted false information about various group members. In an effort to remove their mole, they have begun to purge some of their own people. In doing so, they have removed some very bad men. That part of my plan worked too well. I fear my position will soon be compromised. Now, being undercover means I have no backup. So I must call in a favor, my friend."

"What is your plan to get out in a way that won't mean your death?" John asked.

"I am staying onboard a yacht in the harbor," Vargas said. "If something unfortunate happened to cause the boat to sink while I was supposed to be onboard, they would surely assume I died."

They both were silent for a bit as they considered it.

"That might work," John agreed. The man who had been following us came into the bar and looked around. "We need to think a step further. It looks like we've led this guy straight to you," John said, reaching for his weapon.

"I recognize him. This is someone who works for Ravens Eye. His appearance could actually work for us. Timing would be crucial, but we could use him to take my place."

Knowing the thug had seen us, Vargas hurriedly ushered us back through the kitchen area. We rushed into the alley. The suspicious guy followed us and aimed for Vargas.

In a move I envied, John quickly whipped around from the other side of the kitchen door and used the butt of his gun to knock out the thug. Both Vargas and John had to carry the unconscious man away, but they managed to deal with him.

"Where did you come up with a gun?" I whispered. "You promised no guns, bombs, or bullets for this vacation!" In my anger, I got a bit louder. "Our trip is falling apart. Will we have to leave now?" I gave him a disappointed look.

He spread his hands in apology and said, "Dealing with unexpected circumstances like this is one of the hazards of my job. That's why I always have at least one gun hidden somewhere. You've learned that by now. "

I was about to tell him where he could hide that gun, but my anger was squashed when he gave me the still-unconscious thug's weapon.

He whispered, "Take this. You might need it."

Putting it in my purse reinforced how serious the situation really was.

Vargas took out a sharp knife and cut the bad guy's shirt to expose his back. Above the guy's shoulder blade was a tiny bump. With a small incision and a little digging, he removed something the size of a grain of rice from the unconscious man's body. He reached up to just below his own collar and removed some tape with a similar small object.

He explained, "What I removed was the R.F.I.D. chip that Ravens Eye Group insists must be implanted in their people." He laughed, "They are quite controlling! I will replace his with the one that has recently been removed from me. They will believe I am running and follow. He will lead them away from us. We just need to disguise him a little."

Vargas inserted his chip into the incision on the guy's back. Stomping on the other chip, he put his jacket on the unconscious fellow. We bought a couple bottles of booze and a hat for our "buddy" to hide his face. Vargas poured a generous amount of the alcohol in the guy's mouth and on his clothes. The two put their arms around the seemingly drunk guy to prop him up and move him along.

We all headed for Vargas' yacht, acting like a bunch of happy, inebriated tourists going down the street. At the marina, we rented a boat and motored out to his craft.

Once on board, Vargas was able to take care of dealing with the bad guy. "We must assume we are being watched. John, you and Gia can leave the way you came, so it will look like I stayed onboard."

"But what will you do once we leave?" I had to ask. The idea of a friend getting hurt bothered me.

"It is almost dark. I will be able to slip over the side of the ship unseen. Ravens Eye Group will read my R.F.I.D. chip and go after him, assuming the poor fellow is me. Eventually, I will use another identity to get out of the country," Vargas explained.

John and I took the motorboat back to the dock where we'd rented it. Another boat with some mean-looking guys motored over to Vargas' yacht. They set fire to the craft and it started burning. By then we hoped that our sly friend had made his escape.

We heard a splash in the water, and watched as the unhappy man we'd dragged to the yacht swam away from the burning vessel. The thugs followed, thinking they were chasing Vargas. It hadn't taken the unfortunate guy long to wake up. He swam toward the dock and people scrambled to help him out of the water.

"The more that unfortunate devil runs, the more they'll chase him," John commiserated. He put his arm around me as we watched the thugs tie the boat and pursue him. "I don't know what they'll do to the guy when they figure things out, but he'll give Vargas a chance to escape."

"Do you think we'll see Vargas again?" I asked, as we made our way inconspicuously through the onlookers.

He shook his head and shrugged in a noncommittal answer, "Who knows? You can never tell with him."

After that, John and I were both very quiet as we went back to the hotel. Once inside our room, we talked. "I hope Vargas has gotten away, but how will he get a new identity?" I wondered out loud.

John smiled at me and said, "Don't worry about that man. Believe me, he's got resources."

I suggested, "Let's just get cleaned up and put on something comfortable. We can order room service for dinner. I don't think either one of us is in the mood to do more than just lounge." As I was looking through the drawers where I had placed my clothes, I noticed my things were out of place. It was like someone had gone through them. It gave me a sick feeling.

I turned around to mention it to John. He had opened the room's wall safe, and had a puzzled look on his face. I walked over to see what the problem was. He began looking more determinedly through the things in there.

"Is everything alright?" I asked him.

He answered grimly, "No. Unfortunately, an extra gun and a few other things are missing."

"Who would have known you had those items here? What else was in there?" I quietly asked him, but he wouldn't answer.

"Are you missing anything?" he asked, to change the subject.

I shook my head no, but quietly said, "My clothes have obviously been moved. I feel violated, like the time Ravens Eye got into my apartment."

John briefly put his arm around me. He scanned the room. Removing his arm from my shoulder, he gestured for me to be quiet.

He moved to closely examine the phone and walls. He was checking for any listening devices. I stayed quiet. Then he asked me in a normal tone, "What would you like to have for dinner this evening?" That was his way to keep me talking about innocuous things to cover what he was doing.

The situation scared me, but I answered in what I hoped was a calm voice, "I think ordering in tonight sounds wonderful. I'll take a look at the room-service menu."

He came over and spoke in a normal voice, "I couldn't find any bugs." That was a small reassurance.

"You said you're missing other things. What's missing?"

John sighed, "I'm also missing some papers which allow me to legally function in a foreign country." He thought for a moment. "I agree that maybe we should stick to the room this evening."

Under other circumstances, that might have been fun. John went to the window. When he started to close the curtains, all hell broke loose. The glass shattered and something stung my arm with pain like I've never felt before. The lamp was on the opposite side of the window from where John was. Rather than move in front of the window, he quickly yanked the electrical cord, bringing the lamp down. When the bulb shattered, the room was thrown into darkness.

He assured himself that there wasn't any other threat, and he crawled over to me. He asked, "Are you OK?" My arm throbbed, and I could feel a hot trickle of blood down to my elbow. All I could manage to say was, "I'm not sure."

He moved his fingers around my torso and felt the blood coming from my arm. When he put his hand where a shard of glass from the broken window had grazed me, he heard me gasp in pain.

"I'll need to deal with that wound," he stated in a competent manner.

I was feeling a little woozy and the gash throbbed worse, so he put his arm around my waist and helped me over to the bathroom.

The little room had no window, so we closed the door and he turned on the light to examine my wound. "It's not deep, he said. The relief he felt was evident in his face. He bandaged my arm with a piece torn from the hotel's thin towels.

"I didn't even hear it. Why was there only one shot?" I asked.

He said, "That may have been a sniper that was too far away to be heard, or it could have been a drone." He was worried, and it was rubbing off on me. He looked at me, and gave me a light, brief kiss.

"Now that I know you'll live, I'm going to look around. Stay here."

He turned off the bathroom light and crouched down to leave. He opened the door into the darkened bedroom, and quickly pulled out his gun. I heard him moving around till he whispered, "It's OK. You can come out, but stay low."

I did my best to make it to the bedroom, where I had heard his voice. We heard footsteps coming up the hall outside the room. John grabbed my hand to indicate that I should stay silent. He quietly walked over to the door to look through the peephole, but whoever it was just kept walking.

We both relaxed and I searched for a flashlight in my purse. We got some of our things together.

At the sound of more footsteps, John checked the peephole again.

This time, Agent Smith was out there. She knocked, but suddenly I had a bad feeling. I squeezed John's arm to keep him from opening the door and put a finger to his lips to caution him to be quiet. We both backed quietly away from the door and went back into the bathroom again.

John told me, "Get down into the tub. It might offer a little protection from bullets." He went back to the door to look around.

When he came back, he was unhappy. We both had heard Smith try the door handle to our room. "She's gone now. I want to go check the window," John said, to take control of the situation.

He carefully stayed low behind the wall and peeked through the drapes. Making his way back to me, he whispered, "I didn't see or hear anything, but we need to get out of here. We'll go out the building's back exit as quietly as possible."

With the look on his face, I figured it was better to comply first and ask questions later.

He grabbed my hand and we went quickly down the stairwell. Once outside, we took a moment to get our bearings, then we hurried down the street. We hailed a taxi. John knows multiple languages, and was able to communicate to the driver, "Take us to a nearby hotel."

"So, it looks like we'll have to go somewhere else, but we might actually get to sleep," I said quietly to John. "Although, with the adrenaline still pumping in my system, sleep probably won't come for a while."

He took my hand, and we stayed quiet for the rest of the cab ride. We were dropped off in front of an average-looking building, but we waited till the cabby left. Then John led me a couple more blocks to a different hotel. "I know about this place from previous trips down here. We'll get a room, use a different name, and pay in cash. This one isn't as fancy, but at least there would be no way to trace us here."

The room was modestly decorated and sparsely furnished. John checked the windows and closed the drapes tight. We settled in for the rest of the night. I washed my wound, which had stopped bleeding by then.

"I'll have some food delivered from a nearby restaurant," John offered. To prevent being seen, John told the delivery guy to leave the food by the door. We pretended to be on our honeymoon and passed money out underneath the door. I can only imagine what the deliverer thought, but he was happy to take his money with a nice tip and leave us alone.

John checked around the hallway carefully, and brought the containers of food inside. While we were eating, he gave me a serious look. He was mulling something over.

"I know that look. There's something you want to say. You can tell me," I encouraged him.

He rattled off some names that I didn't know. "So far, you've been lucky." His eyes got sad as he told me, "Those were people who died trying to rescue me, or before I could rescue them."

That bleak statement stopped me. I placed my food on the rickety table and stepped over to John to lend some comfort. I took his grim face between my hands. "You're dependable and loyal," I said, stroking his jaw. "You take duty and protection of those around you very seriously. You've accomplished a lot. I've seen it. Together we'll get through this. I know it."

Wherever that brief touch may have led was interrupted when there was a knock at the door. John quickly and quietly told me, "Right now we don't know who we can trust."

It wasn't clear who he was referencing. Did he mean Agent Smith, or Vargas?

Chapter 16

We both froze as the knock at the door sounded again. Who could have found us so soon? John edged toward the door quietly, with his gun ready, and looked out the peephole. It was nobody he recognized. He motioned for me to move back to the bathroom again. However, this inexpensive hotel room had only a shower stall. I crouched to have as much cover as possible.

We both heard a whining sound outside the window. "It's a drone," John said quietly as he joined me.

"I'm reminded of the drone and equipment we got back from Arty's group," I whispered back.

John got a better look at the menacing thing flying around. "That's a Micro Air Vehicle. It has multiple sensors, and a camera." He explained, "It's usually used by the military. Ravens Eye would use high-tech equipment like this to track someone. It would allow a sniper to get a kill shot from far away."

"They're a more likely answer, since you've been helping Vargas escape them. Surely it couldn't be Agent Smith." I tried stretching my cramped muscles a little to ease some of my growing tension and fear.

"Stay away from the windows. The optics might see you," John warned, and closed the bathroom door. "The MAV has thermal imaging that can detect us without light. It could optically see us through glass, but it can't thermally detect us through the walls or door."

A thought crossed my mind. "Would they already be aware of Vargas' ploy to switch his chip with the thug they were chasing?"

John thought and replied, "Not necessarily. They might be using some sophisticated facial recognition software that started the tracking. That's probably why we were spotted and how we were traced to this hotel."

"Did I cause this by posing as Velma?" I worried.

He answered, "They could be looking for either one of us."

We were startled as bullets ripped through the thin wood of the front door. A floor lamp fell over with a dull thud and the lightbulb broke. The room fell into eerie darkness.

John whispered, "Stay put. They're trying to force us into moving and revealing ourselves."

At that point, we heard an unfamiliar person commenting, "They're either gone or dead."

We certainly weren't about to correct that notion. Shortly thereafter, it sounded like they walked off, probably because the MAV wasn't detecting our heat signatures through the tiles of the shower. The whine from the small drone decreased as it flew away from the window.

I whispered, "Please, don't tell me we have to change hotels yet again."

He gave me a half-smile and said, "It would be better."

We weren't going to get any sleep that night, but I didn't complain. I was moving slowly from exhaustion, though. I could only imagine how fatigued John must have been.

John tried quickly peeking out behind the curtain. I came over to join him and we faintly heard the drone flying around the general area, looking for us. We moved away from the window.

I was scared and asked him, "What are we going to do?"

John thought about the situation. "I've lost a gun and some paperwork. Whoever took them, possibly Ravens Eye, knows who I am and where I work. I'm not sure how this ties in to what Vargas has done, or if there's any connection. For now, we three will have to rely on each other."

We changed clothes and took hats and extra jackets with us. We hoped it would alter our appearance enough to confuse the people looking for us. When we could no longer see or hear the drone, we quickly and quietly headed out into the humid evening.

"Let's follow the crowds. We'll try to merge with them whenever we can," John said.

Every so often, we'd stop at a café and have some coffee to keep us going, carefully scanning the sky around us for the drone. We would put on different hats and tops. We kept moving through the evening.   My training, such as it was, hadn't prepared me for a situation like this.

A few hours passed, and I was getting pretty weary of the hide-and-seek game we were playing.   We found ourselves near the area where we had met with Vargas initially.   John texted his old ally, "Meet us where we met last time.   Will see you there soon."

"Now, we wait."   John and I sat down to catch our breath. He took both my hands in his.   His eyes showed worry, and the creases in his face told of his fatigue.

In his usual unassuming way, he started telling me, "Your life before now, before me, has been structured and orderly.   I'm sorry to change all that.   This is a side of my life I've tried to keep you safe from till now.   You haven't had much field training yet. Maybe it would have been better to have gotten you out of here before things became so involved."

"My life has been more like boring and meaningless," I interjected.

He gaze softened and he continued, "I didn't want you to have to go through this, but at this stage, it's not likely they would simply allow you to get on the next plane out of here.   This is really going to put you through a baptism of fire."

"We've been through some serious situations before," I began to say, but the look in his eyes stressed how bad this was.

He said, "Let me explain.   These guys are contractors. Two of these guys showed up with Arty's group.   All it took was two, and they killed or injured many of my people.   Now they are messing with you."   His eyes showed anger at that.   "You're still not prepared for this level of action.   This is a dangerous situation. Vargas and I might wind up killed.   That's my job and I accept it, but you're in danger.   I couldn't take it if they did anything to you."

"My life before you was repetitious and without purpose," I replied, squeezing his hands.   In a flash, I pictured my previous existence, and how I'd changed and grown.   I never wanted to go back to the way I had been.   I couldn't go back to that.   I was being allowed this one shot to reach beyond myself; to push beyond what I previously thought I could do, and make a difference.

Remembering what Ravens Eye had done to me, I pictured others who didn't have anyone to give them courage or help. Doing this, so that others might not have to go through it, gave me the resolve to continue.

"I'm staying," I said, even though I was scared. "I know I don't have the experience to handle things, but as you said, leaving is impossible. Even if these guys would let me go, not knowing what was happening to you would drive me crazy with worry. As long as I'm with you, I'll be content with whatever might happen to me. Remember," I reminded him sternly, "I was the one who rescued you back in Sedona!"

We both smiled at that.

"The more I think about it, I can't escape the fact that this kind of feeling - what I feel for you - doesn't come along that often," he told me.

I made up my mind and looked at him with determination. "We'll go together, whatever the consequences. I love you and believe in you."

The smile he gave me was one of courage and conviction. "I love you and believe in you, too," he told me.

John must have sensed something was wrong. He moved us both further into the shadows.

"That guy over there is paying way too much attention to us," he said quietly. He stopped me from trying to see around him to look at the person. We hurried down a busy street.

"He probably won't try anything with this many witnesses, but we need to move fast." John pulled me into a run. "Here we go," he said, and unexpectedly tugged me into a dimly lit alleyway. He quickly pushed me behind him while he stayed vigilant in the shadows at the entrance.

When the guy followed us into the darkness and tried to look around, John was able to quietly come up behind him and snap his neck. I didn't like the sound, but I put my hand over my mouth to stay quiet.

The man's body slumped to the backstreet's dirty stones. John crouched and searched through the thug's pockets. He found some papers, a gun, and something else. Nodding, he stood up and quickly transferred the items to his jacket.

"Are those the papers that were stolen from the hotel room safe?" I asked.

"Yes," he said, relieved. Pulling out a pocket knife, he cut the guy's shirt. He felt for the tell-tale bump and extracted an R.F.I.D. chip from the dead man's shoulder, just like Vargas had done. "We'll lead the contractors on a wild chase for a while." We took a winding route back to the fountain. It would have been nice to stay there. The cool moisture and the bubbling sound of the water were soothing after all the running around. Eventually he tossed the R.F.I.D. chip away.

"We need to move on," John reminded me, even though we both needed rest.

Onward, through busy streets and winding alleyways he led us. Finally, he dragged me into the shadows of an overhang in front of the little business where we'd originally met with Vargas. It was closing up for the night, so it was quiet.

"What is it? Are we still being followed?" I asked warily, looking around for yet another threat.

He reached into his pocket and took out that little package I had seen him take back from the thief. He opened it and offered it to me. It was an engagement ring. "We're in it together," he said as he placed it on my finger.

"Together forever," I said, and we shared a meaningful kiss. "That's my John," I told him, "A man of action!" Then a thought occurred to me. "Remind me to check you, *thoroughly*, for any R.F.I.D. chips!"

"You'll tell me if you find any, won't you?" he quipped back. The scoundrel gave me a wicked smile and another searing kiss. I gave myself over to the embrace. My anticipation grew as I put my hand around the back of his neck to deepen it. Just as I did that, someone walked up and cleared his throat.

What bad timing! Vargas looked like an old man, with long grey hair in dreadlocks. A drum with a strap was slung over one shoulder. The man looked like he belonged in a Calypso band.

"That's a pretty good disguise," I said, trying to get my brain to function again.

John smirked a little, eying his friend, but quickly filled him in on what had happened with our pursuer. "There's no doubt Ravens Eye Group is responsible for stealing my papers and gun from the safe. They could have used the gun to kill you, which would have put suspicion on me and the U.S. government. Both things would serve Ravens Eye Group's plans very well," he told Vargas.

That made me start thinking, "Would Ravens Eye Group want Vargas out of the way enough to risk being exposed?"

Vargas interjected, "Indeed. They would be happy to see me dead. They blame me for messing up their operation, as well as for the deaths of some of their people. I really am responsible, but to them that fact is beside the point. I interfered with their plans. Casting suspicions on us would get us both out of the way and give them some time to maneuver. If some of their people have to be sacrificed to achieve that, it would not bother them."

John pulled out his phone and told Vargas, "Now that we're together, I'll contact some of my colleagues and see if an extraction team can assist us."

It was a quick conversation. He hung up and said, "They can't get here till morning. We just need to hold out till then."

Vargas shook his head and said, "It will be difficult, but I might have a solution. Two assets of mine could change clothes with you two and move around in the open. It would create a distraction and lead the watchers away. Staying alive might prove to be a little bit easier."

John slowly nodded his head in agreement.

"In my line of work, I have found it useful to have multiple stashes of clothes, weapons, and money hidden away. They will come in handy now." The suave spy was pretty cunning.

Carefully, we moved to where the new clothing was hidden. We wandered around, disappearing one at a time. We'd change and the decoys would put on our clothes. With our disguises, we looked like wandering band members. We three met again and merged into the late-night crowd of partiers while the decoys went about leading the MAV astray.

We held our breaths to see if Ravens Eye would fall for it. "There it goes," John said in relief as the drone moved off.

I marveled at how far Ravens Eye would go to kill us with no concern about collateral damage. We kept moving and tried to blend in. That was one of the longest nights of my life.

I was worried, tired, and starting to get hungry when I noticed the sun coming up over the horizon. "We've made it! We've survived the night!" We were all pretty bedraggled and weary, but happy to be alive.

John received a text. "It's time to start moving toward the extraction team," he told Vargas and me. "We'll need to keep to the shadows, in case that MAV is still flying around. I've given them our general position. A few members of the unit will start heading our way to assist us."

Chapter 17

Getting to the extraction site was difficult. Fatigue was slowing us all down, though more due to my weariness than theirs.

"Wait for me," I had to tell them when they got too far ahead of me.

There were a few close calls when people took too much of an interest in us as we passed by. For the most part, we had good luck going unnoticed by the people opening up their shops in the early-morning sunshine.

"The MAV seems to be nosing around again," John noticed after a while. We kept to the shade or under awnings as much as possible and tried not to look around furtively.

John made contact with the extraction team. They would reach us soon. At one point, the team had attempted to take down the MAV but it had been equipped with electronic countermeasures to avoid being targeted. The team relayed to John that their lasers were being blocked and it was maneuvering to avoid direct fire.

When he learned this, John told me, "Stay there," and ran to climb up a fire escape ladder.

I knew what he was doing. He wanted to get a better angle, and he needed the drone to come closer so he could take a shot.

He stood up so the drone could see him. "Try to counter this," he said and brought up the gun he had kept hidden behind him. With one shot, he brought it down.

Some contractors started closing in on his position. John shot at them, but couldn't get them all.

The gun he had given me back when we first met with Vargas came in handy. I was even able to shoot a couple of the bad guys. Target practice was paying off.

I was taking aim at a third when some serious-looking guys showed up and took care of them. I started to hide, but John recognized them.

"The extraction team is here," he told me.

I was relieved this was over!

John put me in the middle of the team. We hurried through the winding streets to where the MAV had crashed. Through the smoke, he could see that it was still operating, though unable to fly. That's when he gave it another bullet.

I had to ask him, "Why give it another shot?"

His answer was simple and direct. "I wanted to give it a double-tap to make sure it was out of its misery!"

I could tell that John was immensely satisfied to see the thing finally destroyed, after all the trouble it had given us.

"That's my action hero guy," I said. I was happy that this nightmare vacation was finally ending.

The team picked up the destroyed MAV and we made it safely to the plane. My little cut was bandaged, but there was still no rest for the three of us.

After takeoff we were ushered into a meeting. Agent Smith joined us there. She was in trouble because one of her informants, even despite a recent security check, had been turned by Ravens Eye Group.

I recalled Arty, and John's previous partner. It was all too easy for people to be co-opted.

Agent Smith gave her report: "I had tried to get information that we couldn't get any other way. It was a dangerous maneuver, but I thought that the information we'd gain would be worth the risk."

"That's probably how they were able to link you two to Vargas," someone in the meeting surmised, looking at John and me. They were none too pleased. However, Vargas himself spoke up on Agent Smith's behalf.

"I am familiar with the group in this area. In my estimation, they would never be loyal to either side," he began. "Trying to turn the mole was not totally unjustified, since we have denied them one more of their assets and now more of their organization has been uncovered. Not such a bad ending."

I was glad I wasn't under that kind of spotlight. I've learned that debriefings are hard enough. I hoped that Agent Smith could put this behind her.

When the meeting concluded, Vargas placed a hand on her arm and smiled at her. "Do not worry," he reassured her.

The thought occurred to me that there might be something between the two of them. I didn't want to ask, but I really hoped they could find happiness, too.

Smith said morosely, "I have a lot of paperwork to do, so I'd better get to it."

Vargas watched her leave.

John cleared his throat to get the suave spy's attention and motioned him over. The two started comparing notes. The MAV had been destroyed, and the ability of Ravens Eye Group to cause problems was temporarily curtailed.

"We three are alive to tell the tale and life is good, now that this vacation from hell is pretty much at an end," I said gratefully, settling into an uncomfortable seat.

"Thank you for your able assistance," Vargas said to John. They exchanged a hearty handshake as they sat down.

The suave spy reached over to me. In his usual old-world fashion, he took my hand to kiss the back of it.

In all the moving and dodging trying to hide and stay alive throughout the night, I had forgotten about the engagement ring John had placed on my finger.

On noticing the ring, Vargas looked over to John and back to me. After the courtly kiss, he held my hand in his own. He looked at John and said, "It seems congratulations are in order."

Giving my hand a gentle squeeze, he then reached over to John to shake his hand and said quietly, "I am so glad to see the unfortunate collateral damage remark did not weigh against you. By the way, I know a jeweler..." It's a guy thing, I guess. With a nod of his head to me, he went on to insist, "You will invite me to your wedding, surely? I must be there!"

John was a little taken aback as his friend inserted himself into the not-yet-made wedding plans and didn't know what to say.

"We've only just become engaged. We haven't even set a date or discussed any ideas yet. Once we recover from this trip and put this mess behind us, we'd be happy to send you an invitation when the time comes!" I intervened.

Vargas assured us he would be certain we had his contact information. He left to check on Agent Smith. Before he walked away, he said, "Who else could possibly be a better best man?"

John and I looked at each other, once we were alone. "Who could foresee something like this?" we both said over the whine of the engines.

He looked thoughtful for a moment. Something was on his mind. "It wasn't all that terrible, was it?"

"No, the parts with you were excellent!" I said, blushing as I remembered our shared passion. "Being threatened and running for our lives will dampen things a bit," I hastened to explain.

"Far from your old life, huh?" he chuckled. Then he got serious. "You were pretty good in the tight spots, and not bad with blending in. Why don't you think about a job working with my agency?" He quickly added, "Of course, you won't start off with a field job."

I looked at him and replied, "Hey, now that I've seen what you do, what makes you think I *want* a field job? I'll take a nice, average desk job with a regular 9-to-5 work day, thank you!" I playfully poked my finger at his solid chest. "I also want you home for dinner. Well, most of the time. I realize that may not always be practical, though." I winked at him to soften my demands.

"Fair enough," he said, chuckling. He put his arms around me, and kissed me to seal the bargain.

***

When we finally landed back home, John and I breathed a sigh of relief that we had survived our botched vacation. We both headed off to get a taxi, but this time we weren't going our separate ways. Our recent trials had brought us closer than before.

The various loose ends eventually came together, though it took a while for all the organizational details to get sorted out. Through official channels and some unofficial sources, we learned that Vargas would have some bureaucratic red tape to deal with, but he would be free to go wherever he chose. That meant he would never be doing undercover work spying on Ravens Eye again. I was glad to hear that.

When I asked about Agent Smith, John discretely said, "Both she and I are still doing paperwork concerning what happened in the Caribbean." That incident would undoubtedly cause repercussions for some time to come.

Now, we just had to face planning a wedding. It couldn't possibly be as bad as the vacation disaster. What could go wrong?

Chapter 18

What a crazy and unlikely romance! It never would have occurred to me that some solitary mystery man who was always serious could be my very own action hero. I never dreamed that I could go from ordinary and boring to being stylish.

Both of our lives were altered in many ways. John allowed few people to get close, for obvious reasons. Slowly, I broke down his walls and was allowed into his world. I learned what it meant to John, and what it had cost him, too. Seeing "behind the curtain" had changed my life and my perspective on the world.

Advancement in my training was another change. With more knowledge came the fear of what Ravens Eye was planning next. What would they do with Quantum GPS, UAVs, and stealth capability? Make autonomous weapons? The thought that they could make invisible drones or other weapons that would be hard to counteract was scary.

Despite the uncertainty, the changes brought us together. More than that, I'm just glad we lived through it all! We made room for each other, but coordinating our lives proved difficult.

"There are so many things to be done and decisions to be made, in between coordinating our work schedules and maintaining our relationship. I've met your parents, and when I told my parents of the upcoming wedding, they immediately wanted to meet you."

When it came time for the meeting with the relatives, my attitude of "what could go wrong?" would prove to be prophetic.

I had delayed all I could, but I had to tell John what he was about to experience.

"Well, they're somewhat free-spirited and eccentric," I said, trying to keep things general and not scare him. However, I didn't mention that they got my first name - not the shortened version I usually go by, but my actual first name - out of the Alaskan Water Body Index, for heaven's sake!

***

After we all got together, John had to get over his shock at the nonconformist and colorful style of clothing and less structured attitudes. He told me in a whisper, "Your parents are so different from mine."

I tried to lighten the awkward moment by telling him, "Now you can see why I chose bland for so long!" He adapted, though.

We started relating our plans to my parents. "We're thinking of a small, quick ceremony somewhere nearby."

"Of course, dear. We understand that you can't come back home to have the ceremony. It would have been more spiritually uplifting at our neighborhood meditation center, though. You could at least compromise and have the ceremony officiated out in nature," they cajoled.

"We'll see what we can do. John and I have to stick to our original plan of something simple, unpretentious, and local. It also has to be small to keep it secure. Too many arrangements have already been made to be moving things now," I told them. After that vacation, we had to have more control over the area because it was assumed that Ravens Eye would crash the wedding.

"Please don't spread the news around," we both asked them, knowing that's exactly what they'd do.

"Everyone wants to come and bask in the positivity," my parents insisted. Hopefully, they would stay oblivious to the fact that by broadcasting the information, Ravens Eye could find out.

Enticing Ravens Eye to take the bait was difficult enough. Providing an adequate level of security was harder. John repeated, "Don't give those details away. While we want Ravens Eye to react, we don't want them to figure out what we're planning."

Soon, John's parents showed up to help. "I remember that uncomfortable first meeting. I probably didn't make the best first impression," I said unhappily.

Of course, John compared them with my "unconventional parents." We both had to smile because it was funny to think of both styles having to blend together. "We'll do everything we can to make it work out. We don't want the parents in danger if Ravens Eye does show up, as we suspect they will."

***

At one point, John looked puzzled and tired. He asked me, "Were you aware that both sets of in-laws want an even larger event? We want something just big enough to get Ravens Eye's attention, but this is messing up our timeline. It's also at a bigger venue, further out of the way. The security arrangements are a nightmare for all of the protective detail as it is."

I put my head in my hands. "I'm afraid of what might come next. Even the wedding planner is having a hard time keeping up with these constant changes. Planning all the security details is hard enough. I don't even know what to wear any more. I originally picked a short, simple dress and birdcage hat. They would have worked for our originally-planned simple ceremony. That dress also would have been perfect for any action. So, now what do we do?"

John just shook his head and slumped in his chair. "Every change means another revision to the plan."

I sat in his lap and rubbed his back consolingly. "You've always been the one in control, but preparations are always worse till things come together. The security details will work out and we can look back and smile. After we've passed out, that is! We just have to make sure Ravens Eye believes we're unprepared."

John hugged me close. Then he smiled. "I have an idea."

***

When Vargas showed up and was made aware of our ploy, he was more than willing to let us use his house on Whidbey Island. He even had a yacht tied up to a nice boat dock at the water's edge. I couldn't help but remember what happened to his last boat.

It worked into the plan to have him be the best man, since he had originally suggested it. "It's easier than trying to pick one team member out of all the others. The person selected may or may not even be able to show up. Besides, Vargas owes me a favor," John reasoned.

That was one more problem solved. Then another arose. My mother and future mother-in-law were debating over the style of wedding gown they'd prefer when Vargas stopped by and saw the design I had selected.

"I don't understand what's wrong with this dress. For our ceremony, a short and simple dress works," I said, more forcefully than I had meant it to sound.

"Actually, I may be able to help!" Vargas said. He made some phone calls. When he hung up, he told me, "According to my sources, the most suitable gowns are from Madrid, naturally." He couldn't help gloating a little. "That would be my preference, or Milan, if you must. But the source says to stay away from those French designers. They can only style clothes for the anorexic, stick-figure models."

He saw the distressed look on my face when I blurted out, "I've been trying to lose some of this stress weight. I want to look good for my wedding, but dieting is difficult!" Most men might have cringed at an incipient show of tears, but he bent over my hand and kissed it. He said, in his suave way, "The Madrid designers know how to flatter a real woman. Should I arrange for one to send some designs?"

"There isn't enough time, but I appreciate it. You are a dear, though, for quelling my insecurities."

At some point, things got even crazier. John asked, "Where has Vargas been? I thought he was supposed to be helping me!"

I leaned into him and gave him a quick kiss. "Don't worry. You know Vargas isn't my type!" I put a finger to my lips and thought. "I wonder what his type would be."

"Come back here," John playfully growled at me. "I need some more of that!"

Coyly I asked, "Do you think we have time for that right now?"

Of course, we both answered, "We'll make time!"

***

Agent Smith also decided to help. She suggested, "Maybe you should go with daisies and a country theme for the wedding."

I couldn't see that. Even though John and I wanted simple, daisies and a rustic motif weren't what we pictured. The wedding planner was relieved!

The little glitches that kept happening were keeping the wedding planner hopping. "This will never do." She said, distressed. "Those aren't the flowers we ordered. That dress isn't the right one, and appointments keep getting messed up." No one could explain it and I was stressing out.

When Vargas and Agent Smith started noticing, I couldn't dismiss those things as simple wedding jitters. There definitely was something more sinister at work. I knew I needed to talk to the both of them. Ravens Eye was taking the bait.

"I need to discuss getting a groom's gift," I said, to subtly get Vargas involved. At first, his suave answer was just, "Never fear, you are giving John the greatest gift - that of yourself." When he saw how troubled I was, he immediately said, "Of course."

He and Agent Smith came with me. We used the excuse of finding suitable thank you gifts to explain it. That way I could talk to them privately.

On the way, I asked, "Have you two noticed that things keep going wrong? John's so busy with security lately, I don't want to bother him," I said urgently.

"We have been noticing some strange occurrences, as well," Vargas agreed.

Agent Smith nodded. "Some strange vehicles have shown up, spending time going around the area. Unfamiliar people who claim to be catering help or florist deliverers have been seen trying to get into the area. You were smart to wait to talk to us in the car, in case Ravens Eye was monitoring things."

"John has been kept busy tracking these people down. Fortunately, there are only two ways on or off the island, either by the ferry or the Deception Pass Bridge. That makes the security easier," Vargas said.

I was relieved that John was aware.

They helped me choose a tie tack for my handsome groom. I also picked up a pair of cuff links for Vargas and a necklace for Agent Smith.

"The next item on the list is picking the wedding cake and deciding on the reception dinner," I told them. "Would you both come with me? If you help me pick the proposed table layout, you'll get to taste the food. It's supposedly pretty good," I cajoled.

"I'm very grateful that you're allowing us to use your beautiful house. It has such a lovely view of Puget Sound. It's right out of a magazine, with a picturesque boat dock," I told Vargas as we drove to the caterer. "The island is beautiful and your estate is more secluded. It's the only way John could deal with all the security arrangements. It would have been impossible most other places."

"Not at all, my dear," Vargas said graciously. "I owe John, anyway."

***

We arrived at the caterers and sat down. "John should be able to join us soon," I said. Then I got a text message from him. "He's delayed with more security details. We don't want to upset the caterer's schedule, so let's just start the tasting. You both can give me your ideas," I suggested.

We tried two different meal samples and various types of cakes. As a waiter brought us a selection of the wine to be served at the reception, Agent Smith took notice of him. A person usually looks up when the server pours a pretty generous amount of wine for a tasting. She's so very well trained that most people wouldn't have noticed she was watching him closely.

I saw what was going on, which made me nervous, but I did my best not to show it.

When the waiter didn't leave, she just gave a "thank you" and continued on with small talk. Once he was gone, however, she quietly said, "I'm sure he was one of the contacts in that botched Caribbean operation."

I couldn't help whispering, "What is he planning? Do you think he did something to the wine, and that's why he was being so generous with it?"

Vargas quietly said, "Sometimes it is a contact poison *on* the glass, not *in* the contents."

Agent Smith said with prim satisfaction, "Inspectors are already in place. Tampering will never get past them."

"I've just lost my appetite."

Agent Smith saw my distress and suggested, "Perhaps you should make your selections and we'll leave."

I agreed. I had to make up a reason for not trying anything more at that point. I just grinned and said, "It's all delicious and the presentation is very beautiful, but I must be careful or I might not fit into my wedding dress!"

The chef beamed and nodded at the compliment. I smiled and made some selections.

At that point, we had gotten more than we had bargained for. "I'm going to send John a message that he shouldn't worry about the missed meeting with the caterer. He needs to be warned about Ravens Eye's involvement. I don't want him showing up unawares," I told my friends once we got to the car.

As we drove away, Agent Smith assured me, "We'll look into things. Now, we have verification that Ravens Eye is going to crash the wedding."

She pulled out her phone and started planning for this new security problem, which made me feel better. "We have a lot to do. I'll text Simeon that we'll need to work up a list of trusted people. As a cover, we can add them to the wedding party, since you don't have bridesmaids, groomsmen and ushers. We'll have to get some agents who'd be willing to wear tuxes or bridesmaids dresses for a good cause. We'll also need people in caterers' garb. I'll start on the requisitioning of assorted guns, rifles, scopes, and vests for them all."

"That is definitely not your usual wedding list! John and I had tried to keep this minimal, so we were going to forego a big wedding party. I don't know exactly how you're going to arrange everything for an entire retinue at this point," I said. "I'm so glad for the assistance."

It occurred to me that I still had yet to learn Agent Smith's first name. I didn't know if I should ask, because agents do like their secrecy.

"Security around the grounds needs to be tightened," Vargas said as we got back. "John and I will work on that. You have no need to worry. It is quite possible that Ravens Eye Group wants to interfere because of my part in the Caribbean operation."

So, the wedding day was quickly approaching. Vargas and Agent Smith developed plans for protecting the regular guests, and for dealing with anything unexpected.

I began calling the upcoming date "W-Day" because it was like we were preparing for battle, instead of arranging a wedding! We needed to keep Ravens Eye unaware of our counter-measures, so we could catch them by surprise.

Unfortunately, all these strategies blindsided the wedding planner. "Why can't my caterer's employees be used?"

I really couldn't blame her, though I wasn't able to clarify things much.

"With all the security, you people must be famous, or something. Oh, I'll bet you'll have someone famous among the guests, won't you?"

About all I could think of to say was, "Something like that." Some of the anticipated attendees were more likely to be called infamous. Fortunately, she was discreet and didn't ask any more questions about it. Accomplishing the basic wedding preparations and getting the newly added wedding party outfitted in time took considerable soothing of the poor wedding planner.

High heels and holsters, cummerbunds and ammo clips, and vests for all of them. Not what you usually see for your everyday wedding!

My parents and I were dealing with the cost of the more usual arrangements - food and flowers and such. However, NSA was providing the security equipment and firearms, as well as the bulletproof vests and ammunition.

***

"W-Day" finally dawned with only high haze in the sky. I was nervous, but not about marrying my action hero.

The dress I had finally chosen had a hemline that was a bit shorter in front and longer in back. That was a deliberate choice to allow easier access to a thigh holster than beneath a long gown. The waist was gathered so it would hide the bulge of a holster, too. "Vargas suggested a fitted gown, but it definitely won't work in this situation. How many brides have to make *this* kind of decision?" I pondered.

"I'm still wondering about taking a gun," I confided to Agent Smith. Imagine me, divulging anything to somebody who looks like she could take out anyone with a look! "Should I take this smaller one that I could tuck somewhere? I also have a holster for a bigger gun. Would that be better?"

She gave me some unique insight: "It couldn't hurt to have both. You should keep the smaller gun as a hold-out weapon for your own protection. When you can take care of yourself, you don't become a liability to the people around you."

She softened her usually stern expression. "I'm here to help you and keep you safe. In a situation like this, you never know how bad things might get. You could get cut off from John or the rest of us. You don't want to think about a situation where John has to do a suicide run to try to rescue you."

Agent Smith's wisdom resonated with me. The small gun was tucked in at the sweetheart neckline of my dress. The other one I placed in a thigh holster under my skirt, fluffing the fabric out to disguise the bulge. I had chosen the right gown and everything was concealed. I felt like a badass bridezilla! Grabbing my bouquet, I took a deep breath to calm myself, and we walked out like it was just any other wedding.

Stepping outside, I stopped at the staircase leading to the ceremony area. It was lined with an assortment of white flowers and I breathed in the fragrance.

Agent Smith commented, "I still think you should have gone with the daisies. However, I admit the arrangements look lovely and smell heavenly."

I thanked her for that concession.

She looked me over one last time. At her nod, we started down the stairs.

The bridesmaids stood, almost at attention, at the bottom of the steps. They looked perfect, and there wasn't a holster in sight! The groomsmen, too, were impeccable. I couldn't tell that they had their guns under their jackets, though I had been assured they were also armed.

We walked on. I could see Vargas and John standing there together, waiting with the minister. When they saw me, both of them just lightly touched the side of their jackets. "They're telling me they're armed, too," I surmised.

This wasn't exactly how I had envisioned my wedding day as a girl. *Shall it be small gun or large? Would the bride prefer three-bullet burst or full auto?*

The thought of what we all had been anticipating, and the fear that it might actually happen, gave me a moment of anxiety. I hesitated before walking down the aisle. John saw that look and got concerned, but I just smiled and thought to myself, "He's worth it."

As I started toward John, I looked at the people gathered there. Some of them were familiar. Others were more recent acquaintances. There were many more people in the wedding party than I had originally had in mind. I was uncomfortable with the pomp and circumstance. I took a breath and hoped that the ceremony would go as planned.

Chapter 19

Holding my breath and looking around, I walked toward John. Everything was going well, so far. The surroundings were beautiful, the music was lovely, there were good people around, and a handsome guy was waiting for me down the aisle.

We hadn't quite gotten to the, "Do you take..." portion of the wedding ceremony yet. I thought we might get through the proceedings undisturbed when the unmistakable whoosh from a shoulder-launched rocket being fired interrupted things. The sound brought back bad memories of being shot at by Arty and his group.

A gigantic boom shook the ground and a portion of Vargas' rented estate was blown to splinters. Shards of broken window glass hung in the air for a moment and then came crashing down.

The people who were filling in for the caterers and wait staff had bulletproof vests on underneath their jackets. Some of them ran to their carts, pulling out submachine guns and assault rifles that had been hidden underneath. How they got those in that space is something I still wonder about to this day. Others ran to the refreshment tent. They quickly overturned tables that had been made of bulletproof material and covered with matching tablecloths to blend in. The tables were placed strategically as protection for the guests.

The agents shot at a fast-approaching tactical vehicle, to no effect. Someone hefted a Stinger missile and destroyed the car as it was attempting to maneuver to come around again. The blast caused metal and plastic to shower over the guests, who were being herded behind the bulletproof barricade.

Another vehicle attempted to get through what remained of the front gate. On his way to deal with it, John yelled at me, "Get a vest and find cover! It's going to get in before our guys over there can intercept it. I'm going over that way to head it off," he said, pointing. He and Vargas ran and started shooting at the car as it sped by them.

At that point, things became a blur. A cart had been turned over to reveal more hidden Stinger missile launchers. Two of the agents shouldered the launchers and started firing at the vehicle that was attempting to ram us. The explosions caused more metal to rain down on the scene. The vehicle burst into flames and went out of control. In the chaos, some of the vehicle's missiles went wild and destroyed Vargas' yacht, moored nearby.

Vargas made his way over to me and put John's Kevlar-lined coat around me. "John wanted to be sure you wore this," he said.

"Somehow, John always seems to keep that thing close at hand," I said. I smiled my thanks at Vargas and shrugged my shoulders into it.

I thought back to the first time I'd seen John in it. He had protected me. This was my turn to step up and join him. In a flash, I remembered the times John had expressed confidence in me. Now I had some training. I knew I had the ability, and I needed to do this. I pulled my gun from the thigh holster and looked around.

"I need to get over there," Vargas told me. Agent Smith joined him and started shooting at the bad guys who had been able to get out before the vehicle was consumed by fire.

"I'll back you up," I replied. We ran to get to a better position. Bullets were flying and I saw one of our own guys take a hit. His vest must have protected him, because I saw him slowly start moving for cover.

"I've lost sight of John," I yelled to Vargas over the noise. Smoke from the fires blanketed the area. Multiple explosions and gunfire added to the total confusion of the scene.

"Did anybody realize things would get this bad? Did John know? Don't tell me, let me guess. These guys are more of those contractors, aren't they? Now it doesn't seem like such a good idea to use the wedding to draw them out."

Vargas restrained his temper, and said, "Do you think any of us would allow you or any family members to be endangered in any way? They have all been ushered to a safe area. We just needed it to look real enough to lure the contractors in."

Bullets tore into the top tier of the wedding cake. "Maybe we should talk about real danger later," I replied.

Vargas quickly returned fire at the attacker. He ducked his head but continued, "You are a member of the team, my dear. Never think you are considered any less. Your abilities in rescuing John clearly showed that."

I was temporarily mollified and said, "It's more like hoping for the best, but planning for the worst? Well, we can discuss this later."

Vargas nodded his understanding. I watched him make his way over to Agent Smith. The smoke got thicker. I could barely see the two as they ran to stop a regrouping of bad guys.

Through the haze, I saw John fall and heard him moan. His voice was pained as he reported through the comm system to his teammates, "I'm pinned down." They called back, but there was no response except more enemy gunfire.

I had no idea if he was alive or dead. At that point, I can only remember the feeling that they weren't going to take my guy from me without a fight. I carefully headed toward the enemy location. The smoke was getting worse, but the gunfire gave me their position.

I went total berserker as I aimed the nine millimeter I had taken from my thigh holster. This time, I knew how to put in another clip.

Watching the contractors' muzzle flashes, I made multiple rapid shots. I wasn't trying for heroism. It was a combination of desperation, training, and adrenaline. The only thought running through my head was, "Aim and shoot. Next target. Aim and shoot." It would probably never happen again, but I shot a lot of their sorry butts!

"Member of the team! Oh, yeah!" I cheered to myself when the shooting lessened. Most of the thugs were either dead or wounded. Then, Vargas and Agent Smith fell to the ground. Had they been shot? I wasn't sure. They had become my friends, so I hoped they both were all right. I also had to worry about John. Where was he? Was he OK? Why wasn't he communicating?

***

The unarmed guests had been protected from the fighting. The good guys were regrouping and the few remaining bad guys were falling back. Someone attempted to fire a rocket propelled grenade, but one of our guys was able to get a shot off. The grenade went flying wide. Trying to get to John kept me occupied, so I didn't see where it landed.

"How many missiles does it take for one wedding? I think John, and Vargas, and I are going to have a very long talk." Then I hoped I wasn't being too overly optimistic and my worry for John increased.

More good guys in black uniforms showed up and helped the wedding party stand-ins to assemble the last of the terrorists. A familiar face was among them as they led Bob Smart and the others away, bound with flexi cuffs.

As the last of the bad guys were being carted off, I looked around and saw John coming slowly toward me. His white shirt was dirty and torn where he'd been bandaged.

"You're alive," I smiled at him.

His confident grin told me all I needed to know: my man of action was alive and still in the fight, doing what he needed to do.

We shared a brief kiss and he brushed some soot from my face. "For the moment, that will have to do," I told him with relief.

"Yes. Later," John agreed with a grin. We turned toward the sound of approaching footsteps.

Agent Smith had stayed to watch some captured thugs till back-up could deal with them. Once others took over, she walked over to where John and I were waiting. Vargas joined us just a few minutes later.

I breathed a sigh of relief. Neither of them appeared to be wounded, only a little grass stained.

Smith told us, "Bob Smart had been involved in leaking information to Ravens Eye Group. His updates allowed them to know what the team wanted Ravens Eye to know. That way, we could keep one step ahead of them and find the leak. Now they're all caught, and after questioning, we'll be able to lock up this group. This is really going to put a dent in their operation."

"I'm glad. That's why we took this gamble. By the way, what happened back there? It looked like you and Vargas fell. I was afraid you both had been shot. I'm glad to see you two are unharmed," I told her.

She turned red at my question and just said, "Everything's fine. Now, it's time for you to get married."

To this day I'm not sure, though I could swear I saw a hint of a smile and a mischievous twinkle in Vargas' eye at Agent Smith's blush! It's undoubtedly one of those "don't ask, don't tell" things.

Vargas' rented estate would need extensive repairs. Smoke and flames were still pouring out of his yacht. He came over to stand next to Smith. I just pointed to the wreckage and said, "You don't have good luck with yachts, do you?"

He just made a noncommittal shrug.

"Nothing fazes that man!" I couldn't help but chuckle as the two walked out of earshot.

It didn't escape my notice that he kept glancing at Agent Smith! However, the training I've gotten so far has taught me not to blow another agent's cover. I couldn't help but speculate on the implications. Ah! Romance!

Broken glass and twisted metal fragments littered the lawn everywhere, and the wedding area was a sorry sight. Both the refreshment and ceremony tents were charred and soot covered. Haze still hung over the vicinity. The acrid smell of smoke and gunpowder overpowered the scent of the flowers.

"It's a total war zone," I said, a little dismayed. My dress was smudged and torn. The guests' clothes were bedraggled. "We may have gotten the bad guys, but our parents are pretty shell shocked," I pointed out to John.

***

Finally, the battle was over. Once the guests' chairs were righted, the people started gathering their wits once again. Now that things were beginning to get back to some semblance of order,

I went over to the refreshment tent and had a drink of whatever booze was available.

"After what I've been through, I need to calm my nerves," I said to myself. The adrenaline kick was beginning to wear off.

When I saw someone in catering garb, I asked, "Please go get any unbroken glasses you can find, and take a bottle of champagne to pass around to the guests immediately. It looks like they could use it."

Nodding, he hurried off with a bottle and some glasses on a tray. I called to him, "Make sure to keep their glasses filled till they calm down."

The wedding planner's hair was in disarray and her suit would probably never be the same, but she came by to fuss over me.

"I'm OK, though I'm sure I look a fright," I told her. The woman helped me out of John's leather coat. "I've never seen a more heroic-looking bride," she told me.

"Well, I'll take that," I smiled.

All the members of the wedding party were smudged with dirt and smoke. Some were blood-splattered. The guests had soot stains on their faces and charred areas on their clothes. The large amounts of alcohol that had been passed out had helped the guests to pull themselves together.

Even my parents seemed to be feeling better. They came over to be sure that John and I were unharmed. They both leaned close, in a conspiratorial manner. "We've had a little talk with your fiancé's parents. They told us a few very interesting things. We certainly hope you were planning on filling us in at some point, because keeping us in the dark has us both very conflicted."

I could only look agog at them for how they were taking everything. After sputtering for a bit, I spoke up and told them, "It's called security. We were trying to deal with something like what happened in as controlled a manner as possible. You have to admit, the ceremony is out in nature, though," I said to lighten things a little.

A thought occurred to me. "Since you two are here, and you know about John's job, I'd like to ask you both about handling something like the day-to-day stresses of a spouse who does this for a living."

"Well, dear, you must be careful not to cross waves."

"Cross waves?" Something told me I shouldn't ask, but I did anyway.

"Yes. There will be times when one of you has a low energy rhythm and the other's energy cycle is increasing. Balance is important. Or when your emotions are more accentuated, like anger or anxiety. Think of the ripples in a lake; too many, and it causes chaotic, divergent patterns. Calm is the key."

"It can create dissonance. Match my harmonics to his." It was scary that I was beginning to understand them!

"Exactly! We'll talk later," my parents both promised.

I wondered if delving more into this was a good idea or something that would turn out to be very, very bad!

Stanley and Constance came by to talk with my parents and me. "We're so happy that now our son will have someone to confide in. He needs someone who understands what his job is like and can help him destress."

Even my parents chimed in that they were pleased with the way I was able to help. Converging energy waves and destressing. Imagine things like that actually making sense.

The wedding planner decided to resume the ceremony as planned. "We can't have this event ruined by these unexpected happenings," she insisted.

I was impressed.

"The fuss is over with, so please could everyone get back in their places," she spoke up, taking charge again, and ushering the guests back to their chairs.

John, minus his trashed suit jacket and in his torn shirt, still looked like a dashing hero. Alongside him stood Vargas, who looked every inch the suave gentleman, despite the grass stains on his slacks where he had tackled Agent Smith. Like John, he was also missing his jacket.

Once I saw John, I didn't care about anything else. The disheveled guests were back in their seats, and I walked down that aisle a second time. We actually got to the part where we said our vows. However, if you think that's the happy-ever-after ending, you're wrong!

The minister, who was still shaken after the terrorist attack, stumbled over my name. Yeah, I know. It's easy to do. When the minister turned to me to ask, "Do you, G-Gia – ah... Giahenda Moonbeam Parks, take John Bigglesby Simeon..." John actually snickered.

"You've probably known my full name for some time now, Mr. Know-it-all. Why is mine so funny, Bigglesby?" I demanded, emphasizing his middle name.

He just put on an innocent look and said, "It was the way he botched it..."

"Now you know why I just go by Gia!" I said, giving him a playful poke.

Even Vargas discreetly put his hand to his lips to hide a smile.

I cocked an eyebrow at the both of them. I leaned close and whispered to John, "Be careful; I still have the little gun hidden in my cleavage, you know!"

"Really?" John said, intrigued. That rake just looked down at my bosom and leered! "Remind me about frisking you later!"

It was remarkable that Vargas hadn't lost the rings in the firefight. With the vows and the exchange of the wedding bands, we finally were married! We kissed and made our way down the bedraggled aisle.

Like a general, the wedding planner rallied the members of the wedding party and had them all stand, armor and armaments, in a guard-of-honor line. She even told her assistant to take pictures and make notes. "This is a THEME!" she said excitedly.

I wasn't sure if it could be called "Wild Feds Get Married," or "Conspiracy Theory Wedding," but she liked it. As long as we were actually married, that was good enough for me. She was quite a trouper.

As we walked down the guard-of-honor line, I noticed that Agent Smith was there, vest and all, with the biggest gun. I made a note to finally ask about her full name.

As we grouped together to get pictures, a couple matte-black helicopters hovered over the area. They were there to take away Bob Smart and the rest of the bad guys. A couple military drones were also doing air cover overhead and getting images to document the scene. We were even able to get some wedding pictures with the air cover included.

We looked quite a sorry sight, smudged and tattered, in bulletproof vests, with the air cover making passes above us. The observation helicopters, looking down on the area, got surprisingly high-quality pictures of the wedding party.

Some of the wedding pictures included the military drones doing a close fly-by, courtesy of a couple of John's buddies. The photos with personnel and bad guys in them, along with the helicopters and drones, are restricted and highly classified. That's why you'll never see them. The copies we have in our album had to be certified that they don't have anything top secret in them.

Shortly after John and I finished our first dance and other couples had joined us on the dance floor, Vargas came over to me. He extended his hand in his usual cultured manner and said, "May I request a dance with the bride?"

He twirled me around a little bit. I apologized for going off on him about the mess made of the wedding to draw out the Ravens Eye members.

With his diplomatic charm, he brushed it off as, "Stress of the moment. It occasionally happens to everyone in this line of work."

I wanted to know about the grenade that had gone wide and landed in the parking area. "I heard that a fancy Jaguar had been destroyed. That wasn't your sports car, was it?"

Vargas nodded, unhappily. "I shall have to come up with alternate transportation now," he said sadly.

"I'm so sorry about that. I know you liked your suave mobile," I teasingly told him. "What did Agent Smith think of it before it was demolished?" That jogged my memory and I asked him, "By the way, I keep calling her 'Agent Smith,' but what is her first name?"

He looked very serious and told me, "I have learned that her first name is Jane. She was not impressed with the Jaguar."

"Is that right? Jane is really her name? It's fitting for someone who does so much secret agent work!" I intoned like a famous movie spy, "It's Jane. Jane Smith." I filed that fact away for later.

I also asked him about what had happened at the downed helicopter, when it looked like he and Jane both fell. "So I saw that she wasn't hurt, and if you also weren't shot, then what happened?" I asked in concern.

He smiled, but just shook his head. "Well, my dear, I was just… protecting Jane. From debris, you know."

I noticed his hesitation, but decided to ignore it. All of my adventures have taught me that some things you just don't want to know. However, my eyebrow did creep up a bit at that interesting implication.

To change the subject, I asked Vargas, "What are you going to do now?"

He said, "I am supposed to watch Jane, so I intend to do that."

"Well, someone has to," I said. Trying to hide my amusement, I wished him luck as we ended the dance.

At that point, Jane came up and took Vargas' arm.

John came and rejoined me.

Jane and Vargas wished us well and began to dance with each other. That was an interesting development! "I guess they really are watching each other," I whispered to John.

As the two went on their way, I heard Jane say, "Since your Jag is barbequed, we can use my four-wheel-drive off-roader," she said proudly.

Vargas' expression showed he wasn't too sure of riding in Jane's less-than-luxury vehicle. John and I would have liked to stay and watch this unexpected scene, but we needed to make the rounds and talk with guests.

Eventually, I went over to talk to Jane. She confirmed that was her name. Stranger things have happened.

I had to ask, "By the way, what happened between you and Vargas at the downed helicopter? I actually thought I heard Vargas saying 'I must save you!' Was that really what he said?"

She wouldn't say any more about that incident other than, "I'm just here to lend security support, which also means keeping an eye on Vargas."

"Hmmm.   Well, I should let you continue on your mission."

It must have been easy, since they danced together almost the entire evening.

When it was time, I made sure to toss my bouquet (what was left of it) to Jane.   She and Vargas had become quite an item. It's actually a lot easier saying "Jane" than "Agent Smith," anyway.

Jane and Vargas decided to leave the reception shortly after that.   John and I waved goodbye to them.   We could only look at each other and smile because it looked like those two would continue to "watch" each other.

Chapter 20

In the end, one of the guests actually said that she was going to be getting married in a few months, but she didn't think she could top this ceremony. I guess it's a good feeling to know that our wedding will be the one that is talked about for a long time to come! Guns, bullets, rocket launchers - it's definitely one I won't forget, ever.

The estate still smoked, wreckage still littered the lawn, and the yacht would probably never sail again, but the rest of the guests all continued to party.

While they were shaking off their shell shock (in more ways than one) John whisked me away to a quiet area where we wouldn't be disturbed by the music and dancing. He took me in his arms and gave me a sweet kiss. He whispered in my ear, "I have a surprise for you."

"It better be a good surprise. I'm not sure I can take any more of the bad kind," I grinned back, and kissed him again. Of course, one kiss led to another and we got lost in each other for a while. Finally, we came up for air. Out of his back pocket, John produced some sheets of paper, only slightly the worse for wear. I wasn't surprised at their condition after all he had been through.

"I printed out a job announcement for you. This position deals with information management, and I know you're very proficient at that. It's not any different than the survey data you processed," he continued, as I looked over the duties and experience requirements. "I can help you with the application if you wish, but it isn't anything you can't handle."

"Thanks for the vote of confidence," I smiled at him. I looked further at the stack of papers, but something about it didn't make sense. "Where is this job going to be?"

He smirked, and I elbowed him till he told me, "Don't worry about the job title or the agency. It's going to be in the same place where I work, although we won't be in the same office. We could see each other, though maybe not all the time. We might get to have lunch together occasionally. That *is* something you asked for, remember?"

"As long as it's just a 9-to-5 desk job and you'll be home for dinner whenever possible," I reminded him. He assured me that he would with a searing kiss.

"You're my very own action-hero guy!" I knew he had made a place for me in his life, totally, completely, and irrevocably. Far different from the solitary man-on-a-mission I first met. With what we'd been through, I knew I was transformed from the boring, oblivious introvert I was before we met. I'd become aware of the threats and knew the dangers.

We'd both changed and grown. It wasn't just ourselves anymore, it was us together. Forever. I looked up at him, and said, "Yes," with certainty in my mind and heart.

Then it was time for us to slip away for our much-needed honeymoon. John offered to take me wherever I wanted to go. "We could even go back and try that Caribbean vacation again, if you want," he said enticingly.

"Oh, no," I said emphatically. "The last time, I made the mistake of asking for no guns, bombs, or bullets. I forgot to say no drones. This time, I want someplace close by. No R.F.I.D. chips to extract or electronic counter measures to neutralize. This time, I want some *real* peace and quiet! And rest and relaxation, if you please!"

"You want rest and relaxation, do you?" he asked in a sexy growl. He just winked, "Yeah, like that's going to happen!"

We both just gave a knowing grin to each other. My hand found his. I had an idea what he had in mind. It was definitely what I had in mind, too.